PRAISE FOR JOHN M. KELLER'S WORK

"One of the most original and most brilliant of the new crop of young American fiction writers...Reading Keller's work, one wonders if he hasn't stumbled upon the most poetic and the most profound writer of his generation, comparable only to the South American masters, Bolaño, Borges and Gabriel García Márquez."–*Roll Magazine*

"Surprising, provocative, exquisitely readable*, The Box and the Briefcase* confirms Keller's place as a significant American writer." –Rilla Askew, author of *Fire in Beulah*

"Keller's book, his finest so far, is the most rapturous journey of the senses that the contemporary American novel has to offer. Keller brings to his writing both the dark flamboyance of the Southern tradition and the nimble wit of the North. *Abracadabrantesque* is the most amazing fictional creation of our young century to date. To miss it would be to miss the literary feast of a lifetime."—Carey Harrison, author of *Who Was That Lady?*

"Compassionate, erudite, reckless, and joyful, *Abracadabrantesque* is a work of pure exuberance and John M. Keller that rarest type of writer: a true original."—Susan Choi

"He has written the city's poverty and gore in bold colors and cold gales of anger...Hop on board for *Know Your Baker*."–Charles Bowden, author of *Blues for Cannibals*

"I knew I was in the presence of not just a conscious stylist with a mind well stocked with image, likeness, mashal, but also a storyteller capable, as the best are, of overcoming 'plot,' and turning it into event–a journey not for characters alone but for the reader. I continue to read his stories, each one surprising, and wait for the novels the bio note promises."–Robert Kelly

"Keller's novel delivers...He takes our current-day media obsession with physical perfection a[...] these tendencies have reached [...] ge-turner."–[...]

"A deeply inventive a[...] astonishing grace...if you ha[...] n for a treat."–Jenny Offi[...]

John M. Keller

Johnny Allan

Dr. Cicero Books

Cover photos of Jonathan Duran

www.knowyourbaker.com
www.drcicerobooks.com

Dr. Cicero Books
New York Rio de Janeiro Paris
First Edition
Manufactured in the United States of América

ISBN: 1945766123
ISBN-13: 978-1945766121

johnny allan

ALSO BY JOHN M. KELLER

A Bald Man With No Hair
Know Your Baker
The Box and the Briefcase, the Moleque and the Old Man and the First Coming of the Second Son of God
Abracadabrantesque

For Jonathan, Peter and Sara

1

If you believed my wife, we were all about to get spectacularly lucky. Not the kind of luck that involves winning any kind of lottery, or even an end to illness or boredom. Her prediction was—it seems almost ridiculous to say it—a certain brand of happiness that had to do with the clocks falling back. Her theory was that the world went through a number of different cycles and a new one was about to begin and, when it did, this new era ushered in would be the next great Renaissance—not just for Italy or Harlem—but for all of us, everywhere. My wife was about as likely a prophet as was blind old Tiresias; she's a tall, half-French girl with honey-blond hair born in Balham—her mother was from Bordeaux, and she'd spent her summers in the south of France—who claimed to have fallen in love with me at first sight of my record collection and assortment of pipes. She thinks the popular music is music for children and still doesn't have a cell phone. Our apartment was furnished from every decade but our own—from a rotary telephone to a broken television that sat inside a tremendous block of wood and would require six men to move out. How could she know anything about the future when we lived so firmly in the past?

Anyway, this is what she went on and on about: to friends, when she was drinking, at the weekend as we read the Sunday papers—all of the time. She did talk about other things (this wasn't to say she was obsessed with the future; if anything, she was obsessed with the past—which, she said, would soon come alive again as the soundtrack of the future), and among her favourite subjects were art-house film and American television drama, the borough of Queens and its happenings (this mostly involved music but also men on stoops sporting immigrant fashion and wisdom), "locavore" cuisine, and the Jazz Age and Roaring Twenties. She wasn't pleased with the way that people had taken to using smiley and wink faces in writing (she preferred letters to email), the idea that children could so quickly accustom their fingers to tablets horrified her, and she is the only person I've ever met who's used the telegram with which to formally accept a marriage proposal. Our wedding wasn't an anachronism. We had a small ceremony in Costa Rica on the beach, among a small contingency of friends and family, and then we had our honeymoon in America—and we stayed. And this is where we met the future. Neither of us was prepared for the future arriving as it always has: in the form of our youth disappearing as if overnight, with the nimble-footed passage from one symbolic step to the next—from university to our first jobs and deeper romances on to our marriage and careers, then the onset of our thirties, and the slow, creeping years that would follow on tiptoe, and our replacement with a new, young set, poised to take over where we had left off—but that's what happened. No, the future didn't belong to us. The future always belongs to other people. And to our apartment in Queens, it would send a wide-eyed, street-smart 22-year-old kid named Allan, who looked a bit like Jimi Hendrix.

Allan lived in our building, on the second of three floors, with his aunt and his dad and a sister who must have been ten or so and whose name was Janell. And, to increase his allure, he was smitten by us. We'd seen him before in the building, of course, always crossing paths, each of us to somewhere else—he, most often en route to Williamsburg or Bushwick or any of the other hipster and not-quite-as-hipster neighbourhoods nearby, sometimes with an assortment of friends who were the opposite of what you might expect; he'd acknowledge us with the enthusiasm usually reserved for long-lost relatives, so eager at first to see us that we wondered if something was up, or if he was high, but it didn't take long before we realised that this was just who he was: the most unlikely sort of affable kid, whose innocence was an essential aspect of his charm, but not the only reason for it. We'd see him for a year only in passing—then, one night when we were hosting a large soirée in commemoration of Shrove Tuesday, to which we had invited over twenty friends to share in the British tradition of eating pancakes on the Tuesday before Lent (it's critical in America that you celebrate cultural traditions—there's nothing worse here than "not having a culture"), he turned up ringing the bell to our door with two of his friends: Algernon, an aspiring DJ, and Samuel, who was only slightly younger than us, had four children with three different mothers, had driven city buses for over fifteen years, and still managed to look like he was around the same age as Allan.

We invited them in, and they mixed with the crowd immediately. It didn't take long before Algernon was already offering his latest tracks as material for the films on which my wife worked. Samuel moved in on two of the most attractive single female guests. Their polite rejections confused him—thinking they'd missed his subtle advances when he alluded to compliments he'd received from other women on his smile, he asked them to take out their phones and "type in this number...I'll tell you what it's for in a second." But Allan stuck with me. He was taken by the apartment and my wife's retro interior design. He gushed over our movie projector and asked if we really watched films on it. He asked if he could look at some of the records on the shelf, and then held them at arm's length, carefully reading biographical descriptions that hadn't been read in twenty years, his lips moving with retro pronouncements about the futures of the musicians of the past.

"This is hot," he said. "This is so hot."

When I returned to the kitchen to make another batch of pancakes, he asked if he could help out and, when a friend of mine called from the other room to ask me if I could quickly settle the matter of what had brought about the decline of the British Empire, Allan volunteered to take over.

"So this is all you need to make pancakes!" he was saying to Rachel, a lawyer, who later told me that she was interested in him if he wasn't averse to going out with sexy older women.

The next day he came to the apartment asking if he could help us clean up. We refused, but he insisted. When he insisted again, we let him in.

He told us that he wanted us to be his "mentors," and that he was thankful for letting him come round the night before. He didn't mention his friends. He told us that he loved our sense of style and that he was thinking about getting a record player himself. When he found out that Amelia didn't have a cell phone, he left in a flash and returned a few minutes later with a phone whose screen was cracked, reminding him, he said, of a spider's web. He'd been talking on the phone a few days before when it slipped right out of his hands and fell to the cement, immediately turning the screen into some kind of arachnid art installation.

And that's when the dirty world had come into focus for him. He explained that he had taken the subway home and noticed a homeless guy splayed out on a pair of seats in the alcove by itself next to the door between cars. The man had all of his things with him and smelled of rotten vegetables. And he saw a woman in front of him sneeze into her hands and, only a second or two later, touch the pole in front of her as she exited the train. And he saw heaps of garbage lying in black trash bags all up and down the streets of the avenue, and people walking throwing their trash onto the streets even though there were bins at every streetcorner. He went to a store and bought a gallon of antibacterial hand sanitizer.

"I finally got my phone to work," he said, "but I couldn't respond to any of my messages, so I took out the battery and put it in my closet. And I went for a walk, and it was weird 'cause I didn't have the phone and nobody could get ahold of me. That's the first time in my life that this has ever happened. It's the first time in my life I ever left home without my phone," he said.

We'd never wanted to settle in Manhattan, not with Kings and Queens Counties vying for our attention from across the river (Amelia joked that we'd had difficulty leaving behind the monarchy). In fact, it was the other way around for us; we crossed into Manhattan as if *it* were the *other*, the alternate in the school drama—the real New York was *our* New York, as if all of Manhattan were an extension of its downtown that, having crossed the threshold of midnight, tucked itself in quietly to sleep, leaving its buildings lit as a sort of nightlight for the boroughs. On Allan's Queens streets—streets that for me will always remain dirty in homage to him—we found the New York that we had been looking for, where the subway voices had yet to be replaced by the computerised sounds of the Middle West, where each neighbourhood or store was a microcosm of another entire country, where two a.m. looked like midday in the light of a storefront, in the bustle of the avenues, in the faces and apparel on the street, where personality was not something you strived for but something intrinsic to you, like the unphotographed look on your face.

We spent our first two weeks in New York at a bed & breakfast in Long Island City a two-minute walk from PS1, and then relocated to Coney Island, in Brooklyn, at the height of summer. There, we rented an apartment in a building of mostly Ukrainian immigrants, and were befriended by a couple from Kiev who ran a cleaning business in Manhattan staffed entirely by Guatemalans (they said Guatemalans were the most honest people on the planet). We spent the summer with them chasing adventure, making a second home of one of the beachfront bars, finding our way into the freak shows and the elaborate moustache and beard competitions (in which Amelia, in disguise, placed third)—at one point spending half the night trying to help one of the despondent locals look for his quarter-million-dollar "dragon" (did we hear him right?—this country was full of hyperbole), which had apparently slipped away only to be discovered under the boardwalk itself. At the end of the summer, when we decided to make New York our home, we returned to Queens. My wife fell in love *once*, always at first sight, and she was the type to travel thousands of miles across the world never to stray beyond a single square mile of it. When she eventually bested all other options to play the lead role in my life, I realised that something of this small feature of her personality—of her view of life as at its best either high or low, under microscope or with a telescope pointing elsewhere—extended into nearly every aspect of her personality: we'd travel across town to the most expensive restaurant only to linger for an hour with a single appetiser, or she'd insist we meet at the top of the Empire State Building to talk about weekend plans to do nothing; foreplay with her took either three seconds or seven hours.

And what about me? My name, as it turns out, is *also* Alan (though spelt with one "l")—Alan Carroll. I am a linguist, a wearer of dark-rimmed glasses and smoker of pipes. I work for the United Nations as a translator of German to English. Both my mother and my father translated philosophy and fictions in German to English, but I'm a bureaucrat (it's useless pretending otherwise). I like parties and spectacle and spending entire nights looking for dragons under the Coney Island boardwalk. I'm the one who found the apartment—after Amelia spent three weeks travelling all over Queens seeing flats, I did what I knew had to be done (someone had to be the one to realise she was not looking for flats at all but for stories)—and began asking everyone I ran into if they had any leads. Allan's dad, a man in his early forties with a moustache and a 50s-style hat, was standing in line for a hotdog when I asked him if he knew of a place to rent in Queens.

"I just had a tenant move out of my building last night," he said. "Fled without leaving a note behind, took the lightbulbs with him but left behind perfectly edible food in the refrigerator. How did you know? My God, I guess the people in this town can *smell* vacant apartments."

2

At her request, we set up Allan with our friend, Rachel, the lawyer. We gave him her phone number, and he called her from my cell phone. Because Rachel was, at first, out of town and then, later, extremely busy upon return, it took about ten days before they could meet. In the meantime Allan came round nearly every day—mostly with his friends, but occasionally alone. (He never asked if his friends could come with him—they just all turned up, and it was clear that they found nothing strange about the phenomenon and probably always travelled everywhere en masse.) We'd offer them something to drink, and sometimes they would talk to us, but more often than not they were absent from our conversation, engaged as they were in their own conversations or in a constant flux of multiple conversations over their phones, conversations that did not involve the phones themselves but their various messaging and chatting modes, all of which shared the same device. People's phones had phones inside them. There was no such thing as a phone anymore.

"I met this girl," Allan was telling me. "On the train. She was getting off at the next stop and I had like a minute to close the deal. She told me to add her, but I already deleted my account; when she said she'd give me her phone number, I told her about my screen. I thought about asking her to meet me the next day somewhere, like at a certain time. It was only at the last moment that I thought about asking to borrow someone's pen, but I didn't have enough time. But you know what I didn't think about until afterward? I could have just *memorized* her number."

No-one could reach him. He couldn't use his cell phone to avoid conversations he didn't want to have: with neighbours, with panhandlers, with the guys who gathered on street corners and who knew his aunt, who spoke to him in Fulani. Without his cell phone, he couldn't look up a word or an address. He never knew what time it was. He'd suddenly begun to think of himself as dead, walking around a planet full of zombies searching for outlets, looking for a place to plug into; ironic, because it was also the first time in many years that he said he felt truly, joltingly alive. (And staring into large mounds of trash…)

His revelations came all too frequently, and seemed nearly always as bizarre. Once, he told us that he felt like now he was a bear, living in the forest: eating, sleeping and roving from place to place in search of his prey. He said that there was nothing else to do but watch things happen to other people, and that time itself had sprawled out like in a movie he'd once seen in the middle of the night starring Clint Eastwood. "What was it *like*?" he asked us once, about the time before the Internet, as if he were asking us to describe the Amazon, or the Neolithic Age. (And we're not his grandparents—we're less than a decade older than him.) He told us he was discovering all new parts of his house: new cabinets and closets and drawers, new paintings, new windows in places through which he'd never detected daylight…: "I went into the living room and sat down, and I started to notice things, like a whole bunch of dried red paint at the corner of the wall or a picture of the family from like ten years ago. I don't remember even taking that photo. And when I was in the bathroom, I noticed there was a random map of Puerto Rico hanging on the wall." And he talked frequently about reading books: "You know I always saw myself as someone who read *books*," he said (He always said the word 'books' as if it were in quotation marks or italics…). "Do you read a lot?" my wife asked. "Define 'a lot'?" he said, earnestly. "I don't know…a book each week?" He started laughing uncontrollably. "In that case, I guess I *don't* read a lot. Just articles and stuff. And subway ads. You know, I've never read a *book* cover to cover." He'd already finished high school and had an associate's degree…could he have really done this without having read a single book? *Had his generation been raised in outer space?*

And yet how did he manage to be so charming?

He was to meet Rachel in Manhattan at a bar on the Bowery, for drinks. He showed up half an hour late; he saw her through the window, where he lingered for a moment in awe; in no hurry at all, he watched her through the glass as she sipped her martini—she was "the most elegant woman" he'd ever seen, he said. There were flamenco dancers, and a man with a guitar on a stool, and when Allan approached her, she immediately reproached him for being late.

"It was as if he didn't realize that it mattered," she told us, later.

"I'm sorry—my phone's broken," he said.

"Have you ever heard of a watch?" she said, nastily.

"Oh *yeah*," he said, excitedly, and, of course, the next day he was wearing one, a Timex with bold, digital numerals that he had borrowed from his dad, looking at us through his child's eyes, beholding it—as he did *anything* over five years old—as if it were an antique, a treasure, a relic belonging to a past civilization or species.

"So, do you come here a lot?" he said, after a moment. By this point, she'd already branded the date a failure.

"You know, I went out with a flamenco dancer once," he said. "She was this Spanish girl who'd been dancing for like ten years. It blew my mind how much she changed as soon as she put on those shoes and went on stage. That was the first time I realised that inside people there are *many* souls, or whatever, and that the more comfortable people start to become with ourselves, the more we start to show all of these different identities. And I'm not saying that we wear masks—we do, right—I'm just saying that we've got all that potential inside us, too."

She bought him a drink—had he been planning on drinking?—he started asking her questions about the law, what kind of law she practised, whether she spent time in court, whether she'd always known she wanted to be a lawyer, what was the best part about her job, whether she intended to stay with the same firm, where it was located, how she got there, whether she ever liked to change up her route, what she did for lunch and with whom she ate. And then: what she did for fun and how many serious boyfriends she'd had, why they'd broken up, whether she wanted to get married and have kids, whether she'd like to stay in New York or if she imagined she wanted a yard and a car and extra rooms for laundry or for watching movies, how many countries she'd travelled to, which was her favourite one, how long she would spend in that place if all obstacles of money, distance away from family and language barriers were removed, what she did when she was in hotel rooms (whether she ordered room service), what it was like to be in places for just an afternoon, whether she ever got nervous when she was in front of a jury, whether she was attracted to Alpha-lawyer types, whether she liked wearing suits and clothing otherwise worn by men, whether she ever wore jeans, whether she would like to go with him to West Africa.

"That's where my family's from," he said. "Conakry. Guinea. That's why I sometimes speak Fulani."

"*Fulani?* What does *that* sound like?"

"You want me to say something?...*Jarama?*"

"What does that mean?"

"It means like everything: *thank you, hello*...whatever..."

"Is that what you speak with your parents?"

"With my grandma, and my aunt. With my parents I speak English, and sometimes French."

"You can speak French, too?"

It was then that he leaned into her and kissed her—with his tongue, a passionate kiss that was, she said, premature, unexpected and wet. ("Is that what he does when women ask him if he speaks French," Amelia asked me the next morning, laughing—"give them a French *kiss*?")

"What was that?" Rachel said.

"I just felt like kissing you."

"Ok," she said, in her dismissive way.

It was on their second date that he slept over, at her apartment in Murray Hill. We knew that's what had happened as soon as his father knocked on our door in the morning and asked us if we'd seen him.

She told us, in the kind of intricacy of detail typical to aeroplane safety demonstrations, how things had unfolded; the flamenco spot he had taken her to (which he'd found out about by calling an ex-girlfriend), with candles set inside cubed indentions in the wall; all of the things they talked about; the waiter's own safety-demonstration detail when describing the menu—"The grass-fed beef comes from local cattle, raised in Poughkeepsie" ("Let me tell you what the dinner had for dinner...," Rachel explained)—how he insisted on paying the bill and then, when they got to her bedroom, how he took her on a tour of his tattoos.

"Did you know that he's been married?" she said.

"*What?*"

"Yeah. He was married when he was 19, divorced at 21. He tattooed her signature on his arm. It's still there."

"Did he tell you about the girl?"

"She was a few years older than him, 25 when they got married, the daughter of one of his father's friends back in Haiti. Did you know he's half-Guinean, half-Haitian, speaks French and another African dialect? He lived in Guinea for a year when he was a kid."

This we knew, but it was clear that Rachel, with her probing, prosecutorial eyes (eyes the teal of a peacock's feathers) was gaining on us.

"I lost my virginity to her," he told us when we asked him about his marriage, without pausing to gauge our inevitable surprise. "I don't think I wanted to really, but she was experienced and kept pushing me to do it, so, yeah, so we did it. I didn't really fall in love with her until after that. I mean, again, I'm not going to say I didn't want to, but I just didn't feel like I *had* to have sex with her, well, until after we had sex, then—"

"You fell in love with her afterwards?" I asked.

"Yeah. I mean, at that point, after that, I, you know, I found out more about her, and we used to text back and forth all day long—we wrote like 80,000 texts to each other in four or five months…I started to get the idea that I could be with her. Eventually"—and here he finally looked up at me—"I asked her if she wanted to get married."

"You proposed to her?" Amelia asked.

"Nah, I didn't propose to her." He started laughing. "Are you crazy? I just asked if she wanted to get married."

"Sorry?"

"I mean, I didn't go down on my knees—" He laughed, as if this was the kind of thing that only happened in the movies.

"And then what happened? Why did it end?"

"It ended because I started to look around and everybody was having these New York lives inside restaurants and coffee shops. And all she had was rules about what I could do, who I could spend my time with, and she's the one who put me in school when I didn't want to get an associate's degree in fucking nursing."

"Why nursing?" Amelia asked.

He made the universal signal of money, rubbing together invisible coins with his thumb and forefinger. "And, besides, everybody in her family's a nurse. Her mom and her sister and her uncle and another aunt…She was the only one in the family who wasn't one. She was a physical therapist for kids with issues. I didn't finish nursing, and changed my major to liberal arts" (…an American college euphemism for *haven't a clue*).

But what did Allan want to do with his life? This had come up on numerous occasions before, almost as soon as we realised that he was a passionate soul without a passion, and my wife, in the ensuing days, was constantly imagining possibilities—an artist (but he didn't paint or write), a musician (but he didn't play any instruments or sing…), a leader (but of what, or for whom?...)—"He's got so much natural charisma. He could endear himself to anyone." For the moment, he worked with his father, who was the branch manager for a company that sold electrical boxes to factories, and he worked with him five days a week but hated the job and hated his dad's constant advice about the future, mostly to do with his education and continuing on at a four-year school.

But better things were just around the corner, weren't they? At least that's what Amelia believed…

We were at a South Indian restaurant in Jackson Heights eating curries when it tumbled out—Amelia had spent the past month feeding him morsels of culture: she'd taught him about major periods of art and music, fed him words he ought to learn like "articulate" and "perfunctory" and "nostalgia," took him with her to her Italian cobbler and, because of his newfound obsession with the dirty world, led him to a lecture at the New School on the world's garbage problem (where the detail that he repeated the most afterwards, that had shocked him to the core, was that litter causes fires on subway tracks). She explained that "Don't Mess with Texas" was not perfunctory Texan bravado, but the state's anti-litter campaign. And then one evening we took him for oysters in the East Village, and Amelia unveiled her great philosophy—there was always a moment when she would decide to, I just never knew when it would be...

"Something great is about to happen, and the world is about to have its next great age. It's something we're due. And, if you look around, you can see it's already on its way. So..."—she paused for a second, as if making sure she had it straight in her head; sometimes she was so excited that the whole thing came out a jumbled mess—"nobody realises this, there's *no-one* talking about it, which is crazy, but...modern music began in the 1920s with the birth of jazz, right? Before that, what was there? Classical music. Marching bands. Folk music. Then along came jazz, which ushered in the greatest era of music ever, and then sixty or so years of greatness passed and I was born...just about the same time music—and you might even say mass culture in general—began its spiral into the gutter. Haven't you felt this way? Like it's all just shit, watered-down...rubbish? The incredible thing is that this all has an end date: New Year's 2019...I know that's a long time from now, but it'll be here before you know it—" (Here there was a long, dramatic pause, as she built toward the final note...) "You see, right now all of the great music of the 20s is under lock and key. But, just as the Jazz Age approaches a century old, starting in 2019, its music will be released from the burden of copyright and into the public domain, one year at a time! 2019 will overlap with 1923, 2020 with 1924, 2021 with 1925, and so on...Think about it: the Charleston, 'King Porter Stomp,' Jelly Roll, Sidney Bechet...Satchmo, blowing again. It'll be all around us: movies, commercials, the music in the elevator or the restaurant...artists will be free to sample from it and remix it; low-budget and indie films will use it as their soundtracks; the 20s will be everywhere; the greatest decade that ever was will be back—and the world will have no choice but to surrender to it."

Amelia looked across at Allan for approval, and he gave it to her immediately: "That's what's *up*," he said. He snorted with excitement, overwhelmed by the possibilities...the future that was his fortune to inherit.

And his reaction cemented their bond—no matter how voluble, how forthcoming her nature, even with the ideas that were dearest to her, she expected from others an enthusiasm of which it seemed only she were capable and anything short of a genuine pledge of esprit de corps was greeted as a lukewarm reception.

Over the next several weeks, the four of us: Allan, Amelia, Rachel and I became a foursome to reckon with; we frequented late-night jazz bars and poetry slams and found our ways to experimental and immersive theatre, we hosted evenings at our place with Indian and Moroccan themes and cultivated a vertical garden in our dining room that we referred to as the Hanging Gardens of Babylon (and in whose homage we often toasted King Nebuchadnezzar), we attended theme nights at the Shanghai Mermaid in Crown Heights, for which we prepared by looting thrift shops and theatre friends' closets for costumes, and we often stayed up until three or four in the morning drinking bourbon and smoking bud cultivated in the bosom of the Hanging Gardens, Rachel and Allan hanging on one another in public-private displays of new-love affection that, perhaps because their relationship somehow, for reasons never articulated, nor perhaps articulable, defied convention (for the nearly two-decade age difference? because they were worlds, personalities apart…?)—Amelia and I had a clear taste of what their life behind closed doors must have been like: their toying digs at one another and teasing provocative kisses, his hands fumbling their ways up the back of her dress as she sat just next to him, or on his lap, as he looked into our eyes and lit into subjects and passionate discussions Rachel always harangued as too hipster or too meta-, too cliché or too intentionally original.

Rachel had a way of bringing us all back to reality. One look at her face and you were immediately reminded that nobody cared if you were smart but boring, had travelled abroad to Africa or Thailand or India, had read the big important book or had cultivated some sort of fashionable dietary restriction. One look into her eyes was enough to make you feel stupid for making a joke *you* also thought was funny, or because you were a little bit, unjustly proud that you had the sort of posh English accent that seemed to endear you to nearly anyone else—something that had initially surprised you, that you later bragged about self-deprecatingly and that you were, at the end of the day, careful not to let diminish as you came into contact with more and more Americans who wanted to hear you speak (even if what you said was always less interesting than how you said it). Rachel put you in your place in a way all people need to be: your bluff needs to be called, you are a bit of an impostor, you are not so great. People fell in love with Rachel for other reasons of course (her physique; her smell; her gaze; her tiny, vulpine nose…), but I was in love with her because she never failed to be anyone but herself.

And if this were on offer for free and to anyone, then what did Allan get to see?

What was it like to be Rachel's lover?

3

My sense of morality was always getting in the way, as perhaps it always had done. I constantly asked myself: why couldn't I cheat on my wife? Why couldn't I just have affairs like everyone else? It was a question I asked literally, that the universe took as rhetorical.

God there were so many faces—I'm not talking about the faces of women or men or even adulterers, but faces that held within them the inner character: leery, weary…faces immune to life, to death; some that had written across them such attributes as acquiescence, consummation, pain, freedom from all wants and worries, others full of whimsy and curiosity, and still others displaying signs of perversion or megalomania.

Faces on the train were masks of the ancient Greek variety, and so the subway ride on the 7-line, five minutes to Grand Central, provided only a small window to behold the theatre of the inner, absentee puppeteer, who by the third decade has lost interest in manifesting new expressions and is simply cycling through the same tried and honoured several few.

Every day it was the same routine: I woke and put on the kettle still in the dark; peed, still in the dark; I lay down on the green couch in the living room (salvaged from a stoop sale), and waited. Time passed in small increments. We'd prevented ourselves from buying an English electric kettle (for obvious reasons), which gave me an extra six minutes on the couch. Then came the whistling, and then the noise from the bedroom: *Alan*!

I stood to my feet, made my way over, and then returned to the couch. Minutes later, she came into the kitchen, her sleep mask shifted to the top of her head, put the teabags into their respective cups, poured the water, and headed to the bathroom.

There was no reason for her to wake this early. She did it because I was up and the slightest noises awakened her. The toilet flushed. I stood up, almost as if this was the designated signal, and repaired to the bathroom myself, turned on the shower, washed myself…

I dressed, partially. She sat next to me on the green couch. We stared in the direction of the broken, furniture-like television.

I told her I must have left the kettle on for too long because the tea was undrinkable this hot. She did not remonstrate with me. And then we slowly, somewhat transcendentally, eased out of our sleep and began to converse, having the kinds of conversation we were always having, no matter the hour of the day: discussing grandiose alternate schemes of what we might do with our lives, imagined plots of television shows that weren't on in front of us at the moment, things that had disappeared without funeral or notice (like video shops or long-distance phone calls), the subtle arrival of the next big things (it was during one of our morning chats that I myself first heard of the future of music becoming that of the past), the people around us, our friends, and, recently, Allan and, more recently, Allan and Rachel, whose relationship amused her and was painful for me to watch (I said that I found them too cloying…and then gave her a demonstration of what I meant by this, thus trying to give her the impression that maybe I was actually all right with their cloying behaviour).

She yawned, and so I left the apartment and found myself on the train, boarded the same car closest my exit at Grand

Central and then I walked in clothing I'd worn for many months now, items purchased at charity shops in the UK, at discount department stores in the US, on a few of our holidays abroad, and a superb greatcoat my father gave me (*his* greatcoat) just before his death, and I crossed through streets I had traversed before many times in the same way and that on occasion, in a certain light, gave me pause, in which case I looked around me and thought that on that day I was seeing something different.

I both loved and disdained these rituals. Is it the 21st century man's burden that he is simultaneously always happy *and* unhappy—or is it simply man's? Is it simply mine? I wasn't riding tumultuous ups and downs, nor was I bored or disenchanted or indifferent; I possessed these two sentiments—happiness and unhappiness—in equal measure.

And now, I was in love with my wife, supremely, but hadn't I also grown tired of some things about her, tired of the rituals I so adored, that I couldn't have faced living without? Didn't her most endearing qualities suddenly seem to be somehow didactic? (Didn't it annoy me that she was always asking me to borrow my cell phone, especially when she spent so much time talking about how they were the downfall of civilization?) Or was it simply that I had fallen in love with Rachel, too, and now that I had achieved complete happiness with my wife, I was now looking for *more* happiness, having bit off such a nice morsel of it that I wouldn't have minded doing with a second helping?

None of this mattered. I, Alan Carroll, would never do anything about it anyway. This was a part of my nature, a part of my nature I prided myself on—and hated myself for.

But back to those ephemeral faces of the 7-train—what were they looking for, at, toward...? Did they *know* what they were looking for, or were they, as I was, locked into routine while plying a face that carried on as an avatar, a simulacrum, a simplified intimation of the complexity that lay beneath? Amelia, if she were with me, would point out how many of them were fiddling with their phones, listening to music, in "sleep mode," not present at all ("Look at them," she'd say, "This is why every instance of unreciprocated love is now referred to as 'stalking'; they're horrified by the thought of making contact, even on the most basic level...of even making *eye* contact"), but wasn't this tuning-out also inherent in the human condition? We all become faces on the 7 train at some point. And there I was, among them, malfunctioning, skipping like a record, unable to take my mind off of Rachel and the dose of realism her own face, her own eyes, provoked.

Barely a few months after Rachel and Allan began dating did Allan get a new job as a stock-boy at a discount department store. He said if he continued working with his dad, he'd go mad. There was a certain order to his dad's worldview incompatible with Allan's, and they were always at odds over things that to us seemed rather daft (Allan would get upset that his father wanted him to cook dinner once a week, or at his repeat insistence that he finish his schooling…). Or perhaps they were just a bit too similar or it was simply that the father-son relationship itself was sometimes, for certain people, irksome.

They had a blow-up over Allan's refusal to come home at a decent hour, something that drove Allan away for several days altogether; I came across him in the street on my way to work. He was toting his clothing and toiletries around in some kind of suitcase. "I gotta get my own place," he said, his pupils enlarged, suggesting the energy of future action. "Or move in with Rachel."

"Did she ask you to move in?" I said.

"Nah, but I was just there, and she said she didn't want me to leave. Alan, I gotta tell you…man…"

"Yeah?"

"I think I'm *addicted* to her or whatever. I'm serious. The only time she wants to leave the apartment is so that we can do it outside."

"Where? In the park…?"

"I'm so glad I'm not married. I mean, sorry—I mean, it's cool that you're married. I just, making love with my wife was like the kind of thing that you have to be, like, castrated to experience. Rachel's like some kind of alien sex fiend."

Later that evening, upon return to the building from work, I came across Denis Toussaint, Allan's father, who asked me if I'd seen Allan—"my son," he always said. You got the impression that he might be wary of us and our influence on him, even though he was the portrait of politesse in his nods and his lingering, friendly greetings, this man in hat and tie, with his thick, curly beard that on a much younger man would have branded him a hipster.

I told him I'd seen him that morning but didn't know where he was. Maybe at work?

He asked me how Amelia was.

I returned his question by asking about *his* wife, back in Guinea.

"Allan told you about Mrs. Diallo?" He looked at me as if he'd never considered the possibility Alan would mention anything to us about the woman who'd given birth to him. "She's doing fine," he said and paused for a moment in contemplation, as if he were now asking himself the same question.

"And your sister is well?" I asked.

"Aminata?...She's my wife's sister."

"I didn't know that," I said, pleased not to have entered his son's confidences entirely.

"She's alright. She's doing her thing," he said. "Are your parents back in Britain?"

"No. They're dead actually," I said. "Deceased, I mean. Sorry, I'm not one for euphemisms."

"I'm sorry to hear that," he said.

"I wish they were still around. They were good to me. And they'd become like dear friends at the end. They're with you in the very beginning; I guess that's why it can only feel premature when they're gone."

He nodded. "I know what you mean."

At around half-twelve that same night, there was a loud banging on our front door. Amelia was working in her soundproofed studio, and I was reading in the living room. I looked through the peephole and saw that it was Samuel.

"Is Allan here?" he said, when I opened the door.

"No, he's not," I said. "Would you like to come in?"

"He said this was where he was going to be."

"He didn't say anything to me," I said, as he walked in past me. "Do you want something to drink?"

"A whisky," he said, in what can most accurately be described as an order. "That fool needs to get a new phone. I can't keep trying to chase him down all over Queens."

I set a glass down in front of me at my trolley bar. "How do you like it?"

"Neat."

"So," I said, after a moment, when we'd sat down, "how long have you known Allan?"

"I knew Aminata first," he said. "From school. Allan, I known him since he was 12."

"What was he like as a kid?"

He started laughing. "Rambunctious. He was always running around in circles. Or playing video games…Could you maybe put on a record or something?"

"What do you want to hear?"

"Anything."

I put on *Black and Tan Fantasy* by Duke Ellington. Amelia, frazzled, emerged from the studio and ran down the hallway to the bathroom. This was not an uncommon event…when she was in studio, she got so caught up in her work that she often held her bladder until it was about to burst. A few seconds later she walked into the living room, where she saw Samuel and me sitting. She greeted him and asked how he was doing, almost as if she'd expected him to be there.

"I'm doing all right. Just looking for this kid. We were supposed to meet, but he's off with his woman, I guess. I better be going," he said, downing the rest of his whisky. "It's getting late," he said. "Tell Allan to give me a call."

We next saw Allan at a dinner party at Rachel's. He'd cut his hair short and grown a pencil-thin moustache. When we walked into the room, he was doing a handstand—

"I can't believe I forgot about these," he said, "from being a kid. Now I'm doing these everywhere, like in Bryant Park or on the sidewalk or the subway." He pulled some hand sanitizer out of his pocket and lathered his hands in it.

"I'm partial to somersaults," Amelia said. "There's no end to the fun."

As guests began to arrive, we decided to excuse ourselves to the third-floor terrace, where I filled my pipe with tobacco and we passed it back and forth as if it were loaded with bounty from the Hanging Gardens.

"Hey, can I borrow your phone?" Allan asked. I looked over at Amelia as I passed the phone to Allan, who was busy unfolding a sheet of paper.

"What's *up*, man?" he said over the phone. "Nah, yeah, yeah, yeah…the third floor."

He hung up and passed the phone back to me. "I want to get one of those phones where you've gotta put your finger in the little hole and turn it," he said. "I bet that used to make you think twice before you made a call."

"They were certainly a strong deterrent against dialling drunk," Amelia said—though they were before her time as well.

"Man," he said. "I wish I'd been born just ten years earlier. Don't you think it's crazy that we keep improving these devices to try to get closer and closer to reality—we want more pixels, a larger screen, 3D, but life itself is right in front of us, and the picture quality is…it's *already* 3D!"

Inside the complex the elevators opened and Samuel, Algernon and a few of Allan's other friends had arrived; they lingered on the patio for a while longer while Amelia and I returned to the 21st floor, where the apartment had filled with handsomely dressed Manhattanites of the juridical persuasion.

In her small kitchen, Rachel was holding court with a few of these men: "…I don't like it when people repeat your name to you every time they're talking to you—I don't care if it *helps them to remember it*—or when people use your full name when they're talking to you. This isn't fucking 19th century Russia…" she was saying.

In the living room, a herd of men and women mostly in their thirties and forties stood staring immobilised by their cell phones, their fingers swiping and typing across miniature keyboards. Behind them were the middle floors of other buildings, the lights of these skyscrapers and, in the distance, the skyline that they and their predecessors had helped build and would continue to sustain. I looked for Amelia, but she was no longer in the room. I brought out my own cell phone to see if there were any messages. I had a new, sleek, multi-functioned one. I didn't miss it when I left it at home or when it was switched off, but then why would I do either? I've always loved my phone. It was a great invention, and they were only making them better. And if I dropped it and it broke, I'd just go get another one. Simple as that.

4

I spent the first eleven years in my life in Germany, before we moved to London. My father was Irish, born and raised in Killarney; my mother was Bavarian. They shared a love for the German language, something I inherited from them and that allowed me from a very young age to steep myself in its literature…I read Goethe, Kafka, Freud and Adorno in their native tongues before I'd set off to uni. (How would Kafka have described Allan? Youth—innocent, enviable and suspicious—was so often his subject, *Fleisch geworden*, made flesh, in Gregor Samsa's sister, in the wild and unbridled panther in "A Hunger Artist" or the trusting youth whose bags are stolen in the surreal opening chapters of the forever unfinished *Amerika.*) I never failed to see the world in print as an expression of the German perspective of landscape: schwarz *auf* weiss, black *on* white, rather than the decidedly more stratified black *and* white of English.

They were post-war children; my mother's parents—my grandmother was a baker; my grandfather, a farmer—met during the war, finding love during their expulsion from Western Prussia, like a weed sprouting through the hardened concrete, and so my mother was born in 1951, the flower of that fledgling, doomed plant. She moved with her parents to England in the fall of 1969, and went straight to university, where she quickly realised the tragedy, or disempowerment, of nouns in other languages—that you do not capitalize them, and so something like *die Liebe* could become *love* (also stripped of its article), and the fire-breathing, hissing *der Hass* dulled to the much less sinister, impotent *hate.*

My father she met in Stuttgart in 1974, where she'd been living on her own after her degree (in linguistics); he was there to watch the World Cup, even though England hadn't qualified (incredibly, neither France nor Spain had that year either…). He was sitting, a lone Englishman in a *Besen*, a restaurant attached to a vineyard, eating, and she who rented a room on the grounds, and would occasionally help serve food and drink, brought him his *Karaffe* of wine.

"Schöen Dank," he said, *Many thanks*, followed by a few other words in flawless Swabian (yet spoken in an accent untempted by the desire to sound native), and she looked at his Irish face, his salt and pepper hair (all of which I've inherited), his shoes, his upright posture and George Best hairstyle and pronounced him English.

"Irish, actually," he said.

She asked him what he was doing in Germany, and he said that he'd come because of the lack of an invitation, because he much admired our culture, and because of separable verbs.

"Separable verbs?" she asked.

" 'The trunks being now ready, he DE—after kissing his mother and sisters, and once more pressing to his bosom his adored Gretchen, who, dressed in simple white muslin, with a single tuberose in the ample folds of her rich brown hair, had tottered feebly down the stairs, still pale from the terror and excitement of the past evening, but longing to lay her poor aching head yet once again upon the breast of him whom she loved more dearly than life itself—PARTED.' "

Who on earth was this mad Irishman, and where had he actually come from? she asked herself. How was it that he had managed to make himself expert in her language, which itself was not a language but a riddle, the game of movable type that had inspired the printing press?

He was an auto-didact, my father, an extrovert half the time, an incontrovertible introvert the other half—my temperament comes from him. He'd read dozens of novels in German and could render them into English from inside German covers without a moment's hesitation. Before he met my mother, he'd been working as a bailiff in Her Majesty's Courts; it had never occurred to him that his linguistic abilities could be useful, or that they could earn him a living. My mother gave much more thought to process, to ethics, to revision and authorial intention. My father operated under the impression that translation itself was an impossibility, that the rendering unto language in the first place was just as much a betrayal of the ideas and form, and a quick translation that listened closely and carefully, one that preserved the feeling of the original, was just as good as a belaboured one (one of his early heroes was Sir Richard Burton, who translated *The Thousand and One Nights* in just such a fashion). They both influenced the other to renounce their original positions. By the end of their lives, they had nearly swapped sides—in the course of which they became two of the leading thinkers and writers on the craft of translation, something that, when I mentioned I was both their progeny and protégé, granted me much undue respect from those within the field (especially in Germany, where informal apprenticeship with a master was still regarded as equivalent or superior to the best diploma), and when my father was looking after my mother during her final days, he said to me that that the work of translation is the work of a lifetime, but that he was the text she had understood without thinking and that that was to him the most gratifying experience of his life, a phrase that has constantly resonated with me throughout my life in my various and idiosyncratic dealings with women.

I met Amelia at her flat in Brixton; a friend of mine had directed an indie film, part of which took place in Berlin, some of which had involved extemporaneous dialogue, and he needed me to translate it in such a way that it held as true as humanly possible to the original meaning of the script. The film editor and sound editor were a couple who worked together out of their flat in Dulwich; when Amelia, one half of this couple, opened the door, she said to me, "Come in, quickly…I have to run to the loo." She flew to the top of the stairs. By the time I made it there, she'd already entered the flat but the door had closed behind her and it was locked. She came for me a few minutes later.

"Sorry about that—but you might have been just slightly quicker."

Her boyfriend was caught up in Central London, but she could play the footage for me—there wasn't that much anyway, and she'd key the subtitles directly into the program and then Karl would come back, and if there were any questions he'd give me a call.

"I hate you. To the limits of hate. You're a witch and a trollop. I want to kill you. Brush your teeth. Your dead-pony breath is toxic to not just me but to the whole human race," I said, as I watched the characters speak to one another on screen, before passionately kissing.

Amelia looked at me thunderstruck.

"I couldn't resist," I said. "I used to do this with films, as a teenager. It's really fun."

She burst out laughing.

"Sadly, I think you may have actually improved the story," she said.

Indeed, my dear filmmaker friend had a very short-lived career in cinema.

We moved in together out of necessity, as people living in cities tend to do. She couldn't afford the place on her own, and my flatmate was moving out to live with his fiancée. Her partner moved out, and I moved in. For Amelia, the story of our coming together trumped all those that had come in her relationships before; other details that validated our destiny together kept piling up: she had a record player but no records, while I had inherited a large collection of them from my dead parents (in addition to inheriting their love of German, I also inherited their love for music, especially the jazz of the 20s); neither Amelia nor I loved animals, which had brought about the downfall of several relationships for each of us before (whether you like animals is a question on par with whether you care for children, or God); three or four years before, she'd lived in the building just next to mine in Shoreditch, and yet we'd never met even though we'd both felt in the first instance of meeting for the first time that we already knew each other; we had a few friends in common already (unrelated to the Shoreditch coincidence) and could even recall the details of stories we'd heard about one another before; and then Amelia said to me within a week of her breakup with Karl that for the first time in her life she felt as if there existed a man who understood her entirely and that it was strange because the one thing she'd never counted on was that this could be true from the very first moment, especially as the years went by and the number of people she felt connected to were fewer and fewer.

My parents didn't see each other until a year after their first encounter. My father took my mother's address, and wrote to her for over a year. West Germany won the World Cup—*der Kaiser*, Bavaria's own Franz Beckenbauer, in top form—Chancellor Helmut Schmidt and friends ushered in a frenzy of reform to West Germany, and my father read 121 books in German despite working two jobs to save up enough money for his move to Heilbronn (at Friedenstrasse, number 74, where my first crib was later lovingly installed), where he and my mother were immediately married and where my mother taught linguistics for the years prior to my birth while my father earned his degree in translation. Breast cancer came on suddenly and unexpectedly when she was still too young to die any way other than tragically. I don't know whether my father thought of me as being stable enough to endure it (I've always been of a cheery disposition, but I was only 19 at the time—certainly too young to lose both of my parents the same godforsaken year), or whether I'd even entered into his head at all when after my mother's death he emptied a bottle of pills into his mouth and was dead some hours later. Amelia always said it was odd the number of things we had in common (it's strange the sometimes-morbid content of things people bond over), but that this one was the icing on the cake: *her* mother's suicide, however, was due to depression—not grief, or love—and *her* father was still alive and doing quite well, now living in the south of France near Bordeaux, and making quite a name for himself as a librarian of obscure records: not musical ones, in his case, but those pertaining instead to life's oddities, coincidences and bizarre happenings.

5

Aminata. She wore a piercing through her nose and belly button, jeans she'd destroyed herself with scissors, and brazen, uneven dreadlocks adorned with gold and silver beads that would have identified her at any distance.

"Is my nephew here?" she said, when I opened the door.

"No, he's not," I said. "Would you like to come in?"

"No," she said. "Tell him I'm waiting for him."

"Where?" I said.

"At home."

"I don't know if I'm going to see him," I said, wondering if he'd told anyone in his family about Rachel.

"I gotta go," she said, and flew down the stairs.

Around noon I found her with her niece, Janell, on the stoop, sitting and eating some crisps.

"She likes licking the 'cheese' off her fingers," Aminata said. The little girl looked up at me and smiled in confirmation. "Where are you going?" Aminata asked.

"The store," I said. "Do you need anything from there? More chips?"

"No thanks," she said.

When I returned, they had already gone, but Denis was standing there talking on his cell phone.

He held his finger up at me, in as polite a manner as you can while detaining someone with your finger, and I stood with the bag and turned around facing the street, seduced by the low temperature, a breezy, cool day in a summer of record-breaking heat.

"I'm sorry to keep asking you this," he said, just a moment later, when he'd ended his call. He looked in my direction, but not at my eyes. "I'm looking for my son. I—I understand that you might find it strange that I should persist in asking you about him, but…I've already lost one son. I'm trying to hold my family together here. I know I can't keep track of him at every hour, but…I haven't seen him in several days." His eyes were kind and vulnerable; you forgave him everything because of this.

"I wish I could help you," I said. "But I haven't seen him for over a week myself." I kept from mentioning Rachel; whether he'd told his father about her or not was his business, I felt; or I hadn't considered the question fully and didn't wish to surrender any details without discovering whether or not doing so constituted some species of betrayal. As far as I could tell, no-one was in any sort of danger. "What happened to your other son?" I said, unaware Allan had a brother.

"He's back in Conakry, in Guinea, with his mother," he said. "It's a kleptocracy over there, Alan," he said. "And Binta—that's my wife—went back because her people got power again. They have that better-to-reign-in-hell-than-to-serve-in-heaven attitude. Souleymane—that's my stepson—is a hothead who thinks the world owes something to him, like all these kids today. He was an honours student at Brooklyn Tech. But if you ask me, he doesn't know where he's been or where he's going."

Aminata returned outdoors with Janell, and they headed off to the park.

"And what about Aminata—does she have her head screwed on straight?"

"No, the whole family's dysfunctional," he said, sarcastically. "She's good. She's got a sharp tongue, but she knows how to quit when she's ahead."

"Allan's a good kid," I said. "Maybe I don't know anything, but from what I can see, I think so. My wife thinks he's got greatness in him."

"I don't know about all that," Denis said. "But his mother used to say something like that, often, when he was a child. In Guinea they thought we named him Allah. It's funny how important names are. You know, that's why I rented you the place, because of your name."

The same day, Amelia and I went shopping for earplugs. Queens was loud at all hours, especially if you lived right off the avenue, and the garbage collector came twice a week at just past three (but sometimes later, which on more than several occasions led to my waking at just past three, looking at the clock and, every few minutes, waking again, wondering if he'd already been there, or would be soon…). On several occasions, each of us had slept on the floor in the soundproofed room.

Just as it is for cats, night and day are divided boldly for humans. Plans made in the middle of the night, nocturnal events and observations, in the borderlines of the subconscious, take weeks to become conscripted into the daylight. We wake with headaches and back pain, but can't imagine they have anything to do with the lack of sleep.

It made sense that we would shop for the earplugs together—the major appliance of both of our jobs consisted of eargear. We decided to trot around to the discount department store where Allan worked, in the hopes of spotting him.

I asked a sales associate if he knew who he was.

"I don't," the guy said, heading quickly along his way.

Another, a girl, said, "I think he works in the back."

"There's probably not much of a chance we'll be able to see him," I said to Amelia.

"What if…" she began…

I followed her past the toilets into the back of the store, where there was a massive receiving zone and dozens of employees in brown and blue shirts transporting things to and fro on dollies and large carts. Life was a compartmentalised affair: in every instance of living, there is a front display room, a façade, a market menagerie for everyone to see; behind closed doors, the workshop that deals in creating the illusion.

"Excuse me, sir," she said, when she found him. A couple of his co-workers noticed us and were paying attention peripherally.

"Hey," Allan called out excitedly. "What's *up*? Can you meet me on the other side of the double doors in five minutes?" he said.

We went with him to the side of the building, and he lit up a rolled cigarette.

"I thought you'd given up," I said.

"Man, *you're* the one who got me started again. Then, you know, the hypocrisy of the American workplace—if you smoke, they give you a break. If you don't, you gotta work straight through to lunch."

"We haven't seen you in weeks," Amelia said. "What have you been up to?"

"Just around. I've been with Rachel a little bit. Then, basically hanging out. I went and got my moustache shaved the other day by a barber in this garage," he said, proudly.

"People are always banging on our doors looking for you," I said. "I feel like we've been housing a suspected terrorist."

"It's amazing, man. The lack of a cell phone has freed me to discover and be who I am. I'm rebelling in the most natural way. Can you imagine, cell phones are something that didn't exist fifteen years ago, and now it's irresponsible not to have one! You can't get ahold of me, not through any kind of social media or anything. My friends can't reach me. I don't even have an email address. But all of the noise is gone…" (Amelia was beaming.) "And I figure every year I'll drop another piece of technology, and go further back in time, 2016 overlapping with 1992, 2017 with 1986, 2018 with…what was the year

Edison invented the lightbulb? Eventually, I'll go back to the beginning of time and try to figure out what makes people human."

"Like a Christian Scientist," I said. "Or those Jews whose cigarettes you have to light for them on the Sabbath."

"Yeah, man. Or a Buddhist," he said. "I go on these long walks now, and you know what's crazy? I keep finding money everywhere. Two weeks ago, 70 bucks on Queens Blvd. In broad daylight, with people walking by in both directions. On their phones. In *this* parking lot, a whole bunch of dollar bills and a five floating around a few days ago. And ten dollars yesterday on Havemeyer."

"And then you go wash your hands after you put the money in your pocket," I said.

"Yeah," he said, laughing. "I picked it up off the street."

"What's it like working here?" Amelia asked.

"I like it. I made a lot of friends. There's this one girl…I think I'm kind of in love," he began.

"What about Rachel?" Amelia asked.

"Well…it's an open relationship."

"Really?" I said, shocked. I looked over at Amelia to see if she had registered my disproportionate reaction.

"Yeah. So, anyway, what're y'all doing here?"

"We're here for earplugs."

"Oh, yeah. The garbage truck, right? Three fucking a.m. Home appliances section," he said, as he stubbed out his cigarette and tossed it into the bin. "And keep your eye out for a girl named Nikita."

We headed that afternoon to Greenpoint, where there was a market of housewares and retro threads (three times as expensive as in London charity shops), where live acoustic music poured into the soundtrack; and we went looking at antiques in Williamsburg on Driggs, forever in the pursuit of artefacts to rival a flat we'd been to in Camden Town stocked full of the most obscene and beautiful relics of the past and items repurposed *contre-sens*, where an old refrigerator was a portal into another room and a large ceiling fan, formerly a movie prop, suspended from the ceiling, had been turned into a place to seat four. We found vintage wine racks and radiator covers, industrial desk lamps, glass vials, dressers from 1890, a set of ten bowling alley lockers and even a 1940s eye, ear, nose and throat examination machine. The pricetags were steep. We went to a new favourite bookstore with an exceptional bargain bin filled with tomes that really oughtn't to have been marked down—they marked them down so people would enter the store, but the owner's excessive body odour sent everybody back out into the street. We walked to the banks of the East River, finding a favourite sign, the one that said, "Pregnant women, women of childbearing age, and children under 15 years old should not eat fish or eels caught in these waters…Others should limit their consumption of these fish and eels," and, in case you were in need of further clarification, "Some fish caught in New York City waters may be harmful to eat." We got a pint at a Biergarten that was playing New Orleans jazz from the 20s; the entire band, dressed in period, spoke and interacted—to my wife's utter delight—as if it were the 20s: "Here's the latest from Jelly Roll Morton," the lead singer chimed; all it lacked was the gravel-sound of the record turning around its spindle. Amelia and I realised we were having a perfect New York Saturday, in a city that embraced spontaneity just as much as it harboured idiosyncrasy, to the point that you were always in competition with a previous evening, to break records, the records of the past, the records of the summer you'd arrived. We had tickets to see Antonioni's *L'Avventura*, which would be screened in an abandoned train station near Wall St. as part of the Secret Cinema Underground Series (another thing Americans loved to do—often redundantly—was to refer to something as secret or underground within the name itself: Underground Bingo, Underground Eats, Secret Science, Secret Service: *There's this secret event…*but how secret is it if you can buy a ticket online with your credit card?), and so there we were on the platform of the L-train heading to Manhattan from Williamsburg, and alongside us in full bloom, waiting for the train, a heavy glimpse of the future: a mess of young people none dressed the same, outfitted for Saturday night as if for Halloween or an anti-fashion fashion show (was one wearing a pair of pants with a tail? is it possible to not be a prisoner and still leave the house dressed entirely in orange?). The future was filled with the androgynous, the polyamorous and the redundant—for whom the word "ironic" had been misappropriated and mainstreamed—they *were* what they ate, or defined themselves that way (vegan, pescatarian, vegetarian, raw foodist, foodie, locavore…); they were extroverts or introverts, bisexual or bi-curious, pierced and tattooed where there was space to fill (with photos to document the experience: before, during, after…and then more durings, befores and afters, an endless revolving conveyor belt of pasts, presents and futures, for the archives); when night fell, they stood together on the platform costumed and ripe, beholden to no-one, free at last to pick and choose from the catalogue of experience; by decade or lifestyle, or a mix of whatever tickled their postpostmodern fancies.

"I'm having the best day of my life," Amelia said, as we emerged from the manhole onto the street, after the film, and then she pulled out the flyer for a Silent Disco, in one of the old New York Public Library buildings, where the staff were all dressed as librarians in glasses, their hair rolled up in buns. We went for a glass of wine and some food in a place where you didn't have to move a bookcase to access the toilet, or where, before turning its lock, the stall wasn't a two-way mirror, and then we went to the Disco, where a burlesque act called Rita Men Weep and her troupe performed a burlesque murder mystery to no music and no sound at all, where a performance artist silently screamed and yelled while miming the burning of books, where the librarians themselves turned out to be performers who stripped down to their knickers to a storyline, where the price of admission gave you temporary access to a pair of beat-up headphones that to us connoisseurs held a sort of masochistic allure.

The next weekend we threw a party in honour of the arrival of the end of the summer and the end of my freedom before the Assembly took to the floor and I'd have my chance to cash in on my inheritance in simultaneous translation. During the rest of the year, my mother's attention to detail came in handy as I spent most of my time précis-writing, translating in team or tandem, creating official documents, many of which would never be read by but a handful of people, but all of which would be archived digitally, as everything today was. It was a usual party chez nous, where no-one planned to go home earlier than what would on other evenings, in other places, constitute far too late; an Indian friend of my wife's caused the men to swoon, and even one Peruvian translator to be remonstrated with by his girlfriend when he followed her back to our bedroom, which housed the fire escape, where everybody smoked. She'd brought a friend from Calcutta who now lived in Qatar, and an older friend of mine from the UN named Pramit from Bangladesh furthered the South Asian contingency in a party that spread itself out over five rooms and involved sultry dancing to Bollywood music by the Indian woman and several of the Latinos, intense discussions of politics, art and cricket, and the depletion of my bourbon and whisky supply. Samuel, Algernon and Allan were already fixtures of our local scene and, oddly, for the first time ever, Allan thought to ask me if Aminata could come along, upon Samuel's request. She came and went nearly without notice. On an errand for ice, I walked past the second floor and saw that the door had been left ajar. I'd caught in conversation earlier that evening that Denis and Janell were on Long Island for the evening to see some of Denis' relatives from the Haitian side of the family. Suddenly, the wind blew the door further open and, just as Aminata was approaching to close it, she leaned forward with her hand and looked at me.

"Everything cool?" I said.

"Your party was ridiculous," she said. "Lots of 'cool peeps.' "—she had a way of putting slang in quotation marks so that she didn't have to fully commit to using it herself.

"Then why'd you leave?"

"Fucking Samuel—that perverted little bitch can't keep his hands to himself."

"He ran me out, too," I said, smiling.

She didn't react; she just lingered there. When I came back a few minutes later with the ice, the door was still open. I was a little bit partially responsible for the depletion of my bourbon and whisky supply too, so I peeked in again and saw Aminata, who was sitting by the window, smoking.

"Come in," she said. "I want to show you my stuff." I walked in, and she led me toward the back. In quick sequence, I saw the parts of the apartment that Allan had re-discovered piece by piece after his cell phone had shattered and the dirty world had first come into frame—the cabinets and closets and windows and the family portrait he never remembered taking. It looked like a place where a family lived, unlike our flat, which looked more like a film construct of another time. I said to Aminata, "How long has it been since you were last in Guinea?"

"Not long enough," she responded, quickly, fierily—she had this habit of answering questions before you'd even finished asking them.

She passed me the joint and I inhaled it. It was pure, the way Americans smoked it—not cut with nicotine.

"I think you have a really interesting face," she said, standing in front of me, peering into my eyes at no more than an arm's length away. "I'd like to take pictures of you."

She walked to her bureau, opened one of the drawers and pulled out a stack of five-by-seven-inch photographs in full, blazing colour, striking in what they captured: they were mostly portraits, many of individuals I'd seen over the past several months out of the corner of my eyes—Allan's friends featured in a number of these, and then Allan himself, whom the camera loved perhaps more than any other, or perhaps it was that he knew how to look at the camera as something other than the foreign entity it seemed to be to everyone else.

"I thought you might know something about this," she said.

"They're sublime," I said. "Hats off. You're very talented. I didn't even know that you took photographs."

"My nephew didn't tell you?" she said.

"I wish he had," I said.

A few moments later, I was back in her living room, where I looked over at the chair in which no more than a quarter-hour before I'd seen her sitting by the window smoking; I toted the bags of ice through the doorway. I looked up and saw Samuel on his way down the stairs.

"I was coming to look for you," he said, eyeing me suspiciously.

"Aminata showed me her photographs," I said. "They're powerful, especially some of the ones of you."

"Thanks," he said, dismissively.

We walked back into the party together—more people had just arrived.

And no matter what Samuel might have imagined from seeing me walk out of Johnny's family's second-floor apartment after leaving to go get ice, I still hadn't cheated on my wife.

6

Allanu akbar. Allan is great. The extra "l" that separated his name from mine made them worlds apart, but it was not enough to distinguish us: spoken, even in the highest calibre headphones, you came away with the same sound, and so this lack of distinction was also responsible for our nickname for him, which profited from his resemblance to Jimi Hendrix, and was the result of our inseparability over the next several months; it caught on quickly when overheard by Samuel and Algernon and friends—it was Amelia who had coined it, almost the moment we met him, she said, when suddenly everywhere she went the endless iconography of the original Johnny Allan (spelt Johnny Allen, Jimi Hendrix's given and middle names at birth), on T-shirts and albums, in graffiti outside Café Wha? in the Village or by the subway at Ditmas Park, on a teenager's arm, or in a cake, called to mind not just the man himself but also his 21st century lookalike.

But was our own Johnny A. destined for greatness? He looked the part—wasn't that enough? From Aminata's photos of him alone, you could have sold cigars, war or clothing to the biggest sceptic. Was it his incredible charm, thanks to an inability to pose or posture, an obliviousness to politics and political correctness, or the blush of embarrassment on his face when someone gave him a compliment? (I'd just read an article in *The Atlantic* a few weeks before about how modern American men had lost their charm, how "even in the most casual conversation, men are…guarded, distracted, and disengaged to an almost Aspergerian degree")? Was it that he just needed, as Amelia often suggested, a "cause"—one his own or, I suppose, someone else's? (He would in fact, soon, but we'll get to that...) There was something about him, perhaps something that stands beyond this formula of schwarz *auf* weiss, black *on* white, that I can't put my finger on but that impressed itself on not just me but our entire collection of friends, perhaps a certain brand of originality that had to do with the clocks falling back (yet, of all those who adopted the Johnny Allan nickname, he was the only one who never entirely warmed to it...), or was it, instead, something to do with his lack of irony, something foreign to the Briton that meant that he took the world at face value, as itself, on its own, literal terms? Or was it his late-blooming precociousness that made it sometimes seem as if he'd been dropped onto the earth a full-blown human: unspoiled, prelapsarian—like a child? As we translators know, an untranslatable word is the most interesting kind of word there is.

But what would he *be*? What would he *do*? What *could* he do? Greatness comes in different forms...For his namesake it was music, it was early death, it was a look that sold humanity back to itself, as T-shirts and ideas. There is art: photography, painting, pizza. Science, activism, fatherhood, love...Greatness for an audience of one, no-one or the hundred thousand. Very few people have greatness in them, or perhaps we all do, but very few people live up to their potential. Johnny Allan, on the other hand, just seemed to be more hot on its trail than the rest of us. And new beginnings were just around the corner. Greatness seeks you out, not the other way around. Is that in fact what separated him, when it seemed like all of the other human beings around him had joined the self-flagellating herds in the quest for temporary immortalisation?

And here he was standing in my doorway saying to me, "It's over." He had a look on his face that was indecipherable—What was over? Was he upset? Was he *joking*?

"With Rachel," he said—it occurred to me in that moment that we'd never actually become the foursome we'd begun to be.

"What happened?" I said, inviting him in, offering him a drink.

"Well, she said she wanted to see other people..."

"I thought you were already doing that," I said. "You mean *other* other people?" I'd never thought about how open relationships ended.

"Yeah, well, it wasn't working out, for either of us—except for sexually. Man, I'm going to really miss her sex-pupils."

"I'm sorry?"

"The way her eyes dilated in the moment, like an animal. I've never met anyone so freaky in the bedroom."

"That would be enough for me."

"Would it?"

"I guess not. So what was it?"

"I was too young for her, and *I* need someone who's more passionate, who thinks about stuff, someone who's into the same shit we're into, you know, music…art—"

"She's not into music or art?"

"Not the same way you are, or I am. I don't know if I'm expressing myself well." This was punctuated by a deep, reflective pause. "I want to be with women who aren't distracted, who sometimes have to stop themselves in the middle of saying something to think about what they're saying, or like there's some, I don't know, like they *have* to say what they have to say."

He stayed for a while to wait for Amelia to come home, repeating the story to her in slightly different details: Rachel broke up with him, Allan and she were on different pages, in different stages of their life…the age difference was probably too much.

"Is that what she said?"

"Yeah…I think so, or not like that, but—"

We came away from it with the sense that perhaps Allan hadn't fully understood the terms of the breakup (as so few people do; the whole thing is so misunderstandable), but that perhaps it didn't matter when the end result was what was best for both parties. "Rachel can be so cold, so brassy, so lawyerly," Amelia added. The soon-to-be-christened Johnny Allan contested, "No, she opens up—she can be vulnerable even. She told me about her rough childhood, growing up in the Bronx."

"That's how psychology backfires, see?" Amelia countered. "A byproduct of the sense we think we can make of the world through psychology, and so people think, 'I'll give him my childhood, then he'll think he's seen the backstage.' But there are many rooms with locks on them." (Did this really apply to Rachel, I wondered, or was this just Amelia's latest theory running aground?)

Within two or three days, he was already talking about a girl named Ana he'd met, on the subway.

"You memorized her number this time?" I asked.

"I invited her to a party at Algernon's. She asked me to text her the address. I told her if she really wanted to come she'd memorize it."

In fact, he'd recently become obsessed with memorizing things (he'd also become a proponent of mind-strengthening exercises, and had begun to believe that you could treat illness through thought alone). He read *Fahrenheit 451* and was struck by the scenes toward the end of the book when the bohemian community at the fringes becomes synonymous with the books they knew by heart. He asked me for poems worth learning, and I suggested Prufrock and some short and epigrammatic ones by Langston Hughes (everything always seemed to cycle back to the 20s), but instead Algernon convinced him to memorize *his* poems, poems in rhyme about his heart "aching and breaking and…*slaking*…" (sometime in the midst of the past few weeks, Algernon had gotten a girlfriend, a model from Poland with a pout who was constantly complaining about being bored, and who Algernon constantly reassured with the words, "Hang tight. We're going soon, baby"). Instead of committing himself to poetry, Johnny A. memorized phone numbers and multiplication tables and the addresses of his favourite places, so that when he got lost he could always ask someone the cross-streets (which came in handy when your phone died or was slow and would even save you time looking things up even if your phone was up and running in tiptop shape).

Johnny Allan came to dinner every Thursday, and sometimes on other days, too, but always on Thursdays. I made pizza. (I'd fantasised about this as a child, about a life that included a weekly scheduled night of homemade pizza). Using natural starter, I made the dough the night before by hand (except for the iron, there weren't any other small electrical appliances in the house—Amelia forbade them). I kneaded the dough and then I made love to my wife (the two events were connected), letting the dough sit until the next day when Johnny Allan arrived. And then we rolled the pizzas out one by one, adding the ingredients—many of which were growing in the Hanging Gardens—I added mozzarella cheese and grana padano, artichoke hearts and sundried tomatoes. I'd become fond of arugula. The basil I cut straight from the plant and it was left for last and, cut with gardening shears, it landed haphazardly onto the pizza, spreading sometimes evenly, sometimes not. Johnny A. helped at every turn, made enquiries, memorized the proportion of starter to flour to water to oil for the dough, a recipe that had been in my family for at least several dozen years; and he insisted on doing the washing up and sweeping.

He became like the child we'd never had (we didn't want children, Amelia felt they seemed like too much work, and I could have gone either way, happily), and the weekly dinners gave us a chance to see who he was in a way that was rarely on offer in New York, a city of sprawl, where your friends were scattered about among the boroughs and it always seemed to require extensive planning of myriad inconstant messages to come together, where cancelations were frequent and often last-moment and very rarely offered you this kind of regularity. And so we lived vicariously through his weekly escapades, and we grew excited by the arrival of Thursday for updates on previous episodes, though sometimes we did also pick up pieces on the stairwell or on the street, through Aminata or someone else we happened to come across. We had adventures of our own to which he was always invited, so we saw him then, too, and on occasion we found ourselves on one of his nights, at a family function that we were invited to, or when he suddenly appeared over the (borrowed) phone like a strange voice from another time, calling us to something we couldn't miss, or at one of his regular haunts—one of the positive effects of his lack of technology is that he eventually started to keep what we called regular office hours at certain times at a dive bar in Williamsburg called the Levee, where the drinks were cheap, hipsters were scarcer than usual, and there were free cheese balls.

This is how we met Nikita and Ana and Maria and Tychell and Tatiana. He'd finally captured Nikita's attention when he transitioned from the receiving department to the floor, to great scandal—he'd brought the moral dilemma to the dinner table, accused as he was by his co-workers of being a sell-out, of crossing enemy lines from the backroom full of the anonymous, the unseen, the dismissed, the dropouts, the muscle-bound and the brown-shirted, into the blue-shirted, the college-bound or the with-GEDs, the visible, the sanctioned, the titular, where in his second month he became what the company had identified the "Face of the Month," an award that didn't have to do with any specific achievement other than that you had "captured the notice of the corporation" (so indicated the signed document that accompanied the certificate), and had been deemed "a face to watch."

I was impressed with, and envious of, how he juggled multiple women without moral quandary—it didn't seem to occur to him. He saw himself so clearly in context: "I'm young—this is what I should be doing now before I find *my* Amelia," he said, and I admired his freedom; *all* of his relationships could be open, not closed. This is something that in my twenties had been impossible for me: I'd had a series of long-term relationships, some even long-distance, the endings of which were mostly long overdue. I went from one relationship to the next every few years as if surrendering to the science of programmed obsolescence. When I met Amelia, the central processor lit up, casting off a wave of heat, and the entire mainframe was thrown into overdrive. I knew that I had found not just the woman with whom I wanted to spend my life, but a force so capable of enchantment, that even the most stolid embers of the fire could keep one going for a lifetime. I still believed this. And I *knew* Rachel was just a side attraction.

Still, the concept of their open relationship intrigued me. As a result, I saw Rachel as even more attractive. I wasn't looking for orgies, or even threesomes—nothing too kinky. It was the prospect of two people, once civil and wearing trousers and perhaps something like a cardigan, discarding their clothing and turning into the animals we once were at nature's first huffs of air. There was something strange about the idea that your reward for success in this arena was retirement from it. I'd nearly wandered astray on more than just one occasion but, fortunately, I was always saved by something, and it wouldn't be too much of a stretch of the truth to say that something was almost always me.

But Johnny Allan was still single and on the prowl and, armed with a nickname that matched the appeal the photographs confirmed (let's face it, the name Alan was never much for inspiring sexual intrigue), one late afternoon when Amelia was out of town on a film shoot, I took him to the UN Delegates' Lounge for a glimpse at some of the international girls whom you always see in high-speed, flying past you so quickly that you can only ever fail to see them in anything other than caricature. Johnny Allan never turned down an invitation and, though he never made it on time anywhere (he'd abandoned the Timex post-Rachel, as if the expectation of punctuality were her own, unreasonable invention), he was always up for anything. He was awestruck by everything about the place, from the Niemeyer and co. designs to the security detail, to the history and infamy of the place.

"I can't believe this is where you *work*," he said. "Here, which is *nowhere*"—I'd explained to him the UN's extraterritoriality—"inside New York, but really in some other place, like at the duty-free zone of an airport. But I guess that's true about everywhere if you think about it, because every place is forbidden to someone. Like none of these people have ever been to our house. Nah, but, I could really get into working here, man."

"How's your French?" I said, suddenly jazzed at the prospect of having possibly stumbled upon the answer to the eternal question of what Johnny Allan would be.

"Not great," he said.

"And that other language?"

"Fulani? Not bad, but I can't write it."

"You could study," I said.

"I didn't finish college."

"You should go to college, not even because you'll learn anything, but because people care about that, not just for jobs but for everything."

"No," he said. "College only teaches you certain types of information, and in this country it's a multi-billion-dollar machine. My friends don't come out any more literate. I don't know that I want to buy into something like that."

"I'd like to learn some Fulani," I said. "Could you teach me?

"Yeah, man, sure."

There weren't any delectable young ambassadors Johnny Allan would sink his fangs into; more than anything, it was the United Nations itself (which I took for granted, locked as it was in my "sleep-mode" routine, white as was its colour palette, thirty years as it was removed from the start of our favourite decade…) that intrigued Johnny Allan, its extraterritoriality, its reproducing the same sort of demographics of Queens that contextualised his native environment. It occurred to me for an instant that maybe he didn't meet girls out in the open, that maybe his generation met online, but he later told me that, even in the now-long-gone days when he had an online profile and a body double, he'd never done online dating, nor had anyone he knew even though it wasn't looked down upon—it was simply another destination, another bar. I guess it was *my* generation that had moved online, even though for us it was still slightly on the fringes of taboo—but moving into the mainstream where it would swiftly become the norm, turning, as Amelia would often say, random encounters into stalking, another victory for the designer culture, where everybody was in the advertising business on the hunt for idiosyncrasy…where life was a series of applications in which you were constantly filling in the blanks with your credit score or social security number, or writing a personal statement, or meeting before you met by explaining what you were like in a Japanese tanka.

Visiting the Delegates' Lounge became another of our rituals, and the next time we came along, so did Johnny Allan's personal soothsayer. This time she was talking about Brooklyn:

"In the future, they will only talk about Brooklyn. Manhattan will become like the City in London, the historic centre, the City within the city. It's already starting to become like that. People go to Manhattan for history, to see where the Twin Towers *used* to be, or to see the former financial capital of the world. Everything *today* is happening in Brooklyn: in Williamsburg and Bushwick, in Sunset Park and Do-or-Die Bed-Stuy. Think about it: every little neighbourhood in Manhattan has been turned inside out and stamped with a price of admission: Chinatown, Little Italy, SOHO…; every square inch has been closed off for a film. It's Brooklyn where people go for anything with an edge, where cool is synonymous with Bedford Avenue. It's where people make their own pickles and chocolate and soap, and where they go for nasty homebrew. And that's why *we* live in Queens."

Johnny Allan was nodding his head. "Yeah, Brooklyn's so cool that it's not really that cool."

7

They had become like twins. We were on an open-air subway platform in Astoria—

"Look at them," Johnny Allan said to Amelia. "How many out of 25?"

She added it up. "19!"

"Of the other six, four are wearing headphones."

"And none of them are even using it as a phone. They're all typing."

"Fucking zombies," Johnny Allan said, as he reached into his pocket and pulled out the hand sanitizer. "Want some?" he said to us.

"No thanks," I said. "That'll give my immune system something to do while we're waiting."

On the days leading up to the first great tragedy of Johnny Allan's life, Amelia and he were inseparable. They were always talking about littering in this city full of ironic trash cans, about my wife's belief (and therefore Johnny Allan's belief) that we had it backwards as usual and that only the poor, starving artists should be able to sell their art for money, and whether to put people with cell phones under the heading Zombies or Selfies or Cellphonies or Person-Type Persons. I liked them better each on their own—I liked them each *a lot* on their own—but together they were didactic, condescending toward Americans and America (of which one was a citizen and to which the other had immigrated). At times she marched him back through time like someone giving a walking tour of the past—"Imagine what it used to be like. The people on the streets had no choice but to look around: what else would you do with no phone in your hands or against your ears? It was much easier to avoid confusion. In order to talk to someone, you couldn't text. You had no choice but to ring them or go round to theirs. You were forced to plan ahead, to say, I'm going to meet you here at such-and-such time…" It got to the point where, when my wife talked about the glittering lights of the future, about the past and present and future all becoming as one, I began to tune them out, or I said something with no apparent relevance, like "When was the last time we did laundry?" or I played devil's advocate: "Will it *really* be that different, when all of this music goes into the public domain?", which was a statement verging on sacrilege and infidelity, and was excused perhaps only because even they must have known that someone had to play that role. Left to their own devices, I'd begun to think they'd turn into a two-person cult.

People were stopping by our flat to see Johnny Allan with increasing regularity (which turned into messages recorded on a message board I'd installed myself next to the door…). I constantly fielded phone calls from the Algernons of his set, from Nikita (whose face and voice were incompatible, a sultry vixen with a nine year old's pitch), from his co-workers (both the blues and the browns), from Aminata and, once, his dentist's office, phoning to remind about an appointment. Among the many things that Johnny Allan lacked—which included a sense of irony—perhaps his best and worst quality were wrapped up in the same duplicitous trait: the ability to befriend and create instant solidarity and the appearance of lifelong friendship with absolutely anyone, and a lack of discretion in choosing said friends. No-one got the benefit of the doubt because there was no initial doubt; Johnny Allan befriended the entire human circus.

One day his father appeared at the door, his suit drenched by rain, a hopelessness in his voice. "Can you tell him to call his mother," he said. "His mother has some news." Johnny Allan didn't appear for another day—he'd just started seeing a new girl, an NYU student named Trisha. He'd met her at the Levee; he'd been waiting for her to be alone so that he could talk to her, and then finally her friend went to the bathroom, and she immediately pulled out her cell phone. "I've been listening to your whole conversation," he said. "But you'll never meet a guy if you act like a Selfie," he said and, thanks to their ensuing spat, he'd since slept over several nights at hers in student housing. When he arrived home, everyone was gone from the house, the door was locked, and he didn't have a key—he hadn't had one in years. "There's always somebody here," he said, panicking—it was the first time I'd ever seen him panic—"I can't believe they left and locked the door."

Using a separate, interior staircase that connected our apartments, which we used as a storage area and which was full of anything we and the Toussaint-Diallo clan didn't have space to store inside the apartment, Johnny Allan shimmied down the banister, mindful not to fall into the appliances and mattresses and other artefacts blocking the way, and managed to reach the second-floor door, which was locked but that he managed to force open with a screwdriver and his New York State ID, which he'd nearly destroyed in the process. Once inside, he found his mother's phone number and called from his father's computer, but there was no answer. It was only at this moment that it occurred to him to call his father.

It went straight to voicemail.

And Aminata?

It rang five times, and there was her voice: "Call me back later, y'all; I never check my voicemail. Just being honest..."

She rang him back a few minutes later, saying she didn't know anything, but that she had a missed call from Denis.

An hour or so passed in which the apartment had turned, the door between our worlds unlocked and open, into the house it had once been in its original design.

Finally, Johnny Allan called his mother again from our computer, and suddenly on the screen there appeared the frozen image of a woman in her 40s wearing a headwrap and an expression on her face of paranormal consternation that remained on her face throughout the entire call.

He spoke to her in a stream of words in Fulani, and she responded, and then he started laughing, with tears in his eyes, and Amelia and I looked at one another spellbound.

When he finally hung up, he said, his eyes bright red, "My mom and brother are coming in December, around Christmastime."

Later that week Johnny Allan was at the Levee with Jean-David, a burly Haitian man around his age who worked security at the department store, talking with two girls from Queens whom they'd met at the bar, whose phone numbers they'd just taken, one of whose Johnny had memorized ("Don't tell me you're afraid to show me your phone because it's like three years old," one of the girls said. "Nah, I ain't got a phone," Johnny said. "I mean, I'm a conscientious objector"), when suddenly from behind him there was some commotion and a bowl full of cheese balls soared into the air and from that direction he said he saw a fist flying and then he watched as that fist was deflected and the guy to whom the fist belonged was pulled to the floor. The girl he'd been talking to screamed—"What the fuck are you doing here, *coño*!" "Who is this nigger you're talking to?" the guy, who was quick to his feet, said. "I'm not your girlfriend," she said, "I'm not even your mother," and that's when the guy threw another punch at Johnny that was, once again, deflected by Jean-David ("It's a lot like having your own personal bouncer," Johnny said, the next Thursday, when narrating the story to us.) Another guy tried to clock Johnny from behind, but by then he knew what was going on, and he pushed himself off the barstool and got out of the way as Jean-David popped the guy in the face with his fist, sending him sailing down to the ground. By then, the bouncers of the bar had arrived and took everyone outside, where Johnny Allan persuaded them to let him and Jean-David back in. The girls left with the two guys, but Johnny Allan and Jean-David continued to sit at the bar and talk about what had just happened with the bartender, who gave them the rest of their drinks on the house for the rest of the night.

On Thanksgiving, our favourite American holiday, we were invited by Denis Toussaint to dinner at three in the afternoon for the typical spread of turkey, mashed potatoes, green bean casserole, stuffing, sweet potatoes, cranberry sauce and an assembly of pies—traditional fare that arrives once a year and then disappears from memory as soon as Americans are asked by foreigners like us, *So what* is *American food...? No, not hamburgers...The name of a German town actually takes up most of the word, you see? Like the frankfurter is from Frankfurt and Berliner doughnuts come from Berlin? You can't claim pizza as yours, obviously, either. And French fries...don't get me started...*

It was the first time we'd all sat down to dine together: Denis, Aminata, Johnny Allan, Janell, Amelia and I, along with a slew of other Toussaints, all second- and third-generation Haitians, uncles and aunts and cousins who mostly lived on Long Island or Queens and the Bronx and who sometimes spoke Creole, which Johnny and Janell understood, but didn't speak, and they spoke a mix of English and French to Aminata (whose French was extremely posh, according to Amelia). "Things haven't been right since Guinea," they said, teasing their brother…The story of his instant infatuation with Binta, their rapid engagement, her pregnancy and then their separation, suggested a Denis that may have once been the prototype for future Toussaints.

Before the turkey was cut, we sat at a large table in the living room and went around the room, each saying a few words of thanks, something Janell had instigated, having done it the day before at her school. What followed was a touching, humbling array of thanks-givings from people who spoke sincerely while looking down at the floor in embarrassment, almost as if these were dark, horrible confessions: for health, family, friendship, love, companionship, employment, support, trust and faith. Amelia, who'd endeared herself to everyone so swiftly it was as if she were a long-lost cousin, said, "I'm thankful to have been invited here by you, Denis, and—

though we should do, we don't have any kind of similar tradition in Britain, because it's you sincere American folks who've created the Lifetime network and Hallmark cards and only us Brits who know how to say they love each other so subtly it's usually confused with something else. I'm grateful that your Allan has come into our lives and become our friend, and I'm especially grateful for my husband. Even though he boils the tea for too long and slurps his cereal, he's like a secret only I get to know about, and life with him is a series of delectable adventures. I love you, Alan-One-El."

It was when we had retired to the living room to watch the Giants and Jets play that Janell, her face turning red, stumbled into the living room and fell to the floor. At first, no-one knew what was wrong, but an older cousin yelled out, "She's choking!" Denis' sister swept to her feet, pressed her fingers into Janell's stomach, and the bone flew out of her mouth instantly, the whole event unfolding all in a matter of seconds.

That evening Johnny Allan reported to the discount department store for the Black Friday shift that required that everyone be on the floor by ten. Displays were built, signs indicating bargains were strewn throughout—there were DVDs for a dollar, flatscreen TVs marked down to close to a third-off, digital cameras, memory cards, mini-refrigerators and microwaves, blenders and washing machines and rice cookers, a "nostalgic" electric plastic bucket ice cream maker, a make-your-own-fizzy-drink kit, air conditioners and coffee foamers and odour-eliminating vacuum bags, pizza stones and cell phones and guns and security cabinets and backpacks and flashlights and jewellery, all slashed down considerably below standard retail price. Johnny Allan and Nikita worked as a team, he following the diagrams from the corporate offices detailing the anatomy of the display, the two of them together building the case, she adding her own flourish because *who would know?*, and in the chaos of the first hours of Friday nothing they set up would still be standing, a thought which she said excited her.

At a quarter to eleven, they walked to the front of the store, where Johnny Allan saw Jean-David, who pointed at the throngs of shoppers on the other side of the doors, saying that this would definitely be the most excitement he'd have all year when they opened the doors and the customers stampeded through. Johnny went to the back of the store, back into the brown-shirted zone, slipped out into the street and rolled a cigarette. He lingered longer than usual, said he got caught up in thoughts of marriage to Nikita and the children they would have, when midnight struck and Black Friday began.

When he went back into the store, the shoppers had already been unleashed; he was reminded of a game show he'd seen where customers are let loose with a shopping cart and told they could fill their baskets with as much as they liked so long as the total didn't exceed $500. He stood back and watched, gave directions toward the electronics and home appliances sections, and giggled to himself—he was a little bit high, actually—about how ridiculous all of these people were, and then he wandered over, trying to get out of the way of customers dashing across the store with their carts, in search of Nikita, who was meant to be in the cosmetics section.

She wasn't. She was in the front of the store yelling and screaming as Jean-David lay immobile on the ground a dozen or so feet from the front door, now surrounded by store employees and the assistant manager and a nurse who emerged from the crowd. The ground was littered in glass where the doors to the store had shattered and, seeing this, Nikita at first worried he'd been struck by a stray piece. The paramedics quickly arrived and put him on a stretcher and he was taken through the same doors through which the customers had come just a few minutes before. A few hours later Nikita got a text from the assistant manager that said, "Jean-David is no longer with us :(", the cause of death: asphyxiation, or, more to the point: he'd been trampled to death by several hundred customers who, having removed the hinges of the doors of the store and penetrated the human and metal barricades put into place to slow them, rushed through and knocked him down and then, as he struggled for breath, walked over and on top of him, killing him with their feet.

Walking through Queens the next day, Johnny Allan saw a woman carrying a cell phone approaching him without slowing or noticing that he was in her direct path. He stood still and waited for her to walk straight into him at such a speed that, when she did, her cell phone dropped out of her hands and smashed into the sidewalk.

"What the fuck!" she cried out. "Why did you let me walk right into you?"

"Fucking Zombie," he said, continuing on his way. He thought: She'll just go replace it, and she won't learn her lesson. It's a rare case that, because of a shattered cell phone screen, a person can recover his or her birthright, and begin to live a different life.

In this respect, Johnny Allan was certainly unusual.

8

It was difficult not to be completely mesmerized by the transformation. First, a van showed up. From the window, you saw first the children, the two of them—Zeinab, the girl, who was six; Allan, the seven-year-old boy (named after his uncle)—who sprang from the vehicle as if from the starting gate at a racetrack; then Mariama, Souleymane's wife, bejewelled, her hair in a wrap, her dress aswirl with polygonal ankara prints; next Souleymane himself in sunglasses; and finally Binta, Aminata's sister, Johnny Allan's mother, a tall, serious woman wearing a majestic purple grand boubou and headwrap. The outfits, the order of egress, the look on the adults' faces, as if New York air was contaminated—it gave the family an immediate air of superiority that, like the sudden arrival of a new season, converted everything that was comprehensible into something abstract and, where things were once misunderstood or unintelligible, the Guinea contingency cleared it all up. *Things haven't been right since Guinea,* I remembered one of Denis' family members saying.

But *which* Guinea was their Guinea? It seemed this was always the question; informed people nodded their head pretending they could delineate the differences among them, but there were 13 variations on the theme (Papua New Guinea, Guinea-Bissau, Equatorial Guinea…) now or in history (not to mention the pig and the coin). (Nowadays I often suggest, anytime anyone doesn't know what to name something, that they call it Guinea.) I didn't see Denis kiss his wife or anyone else, and he shook his stepson's hand, but Aminata buried her sister in hugs and kissed the children and her nephew as Denis and Souleymane brought the bags into the house.

Johnny Allan wasn't home. He hadn't been about much at all in the past month, and there wasn't any way of getting ahold of him. He spent most of his time with Nikita (the only human being he said he could face seeing, a girl whom he'd also convinced to stop using; "*Drugs*?" "No, *phones*, man") at her parents' on Long Island, and when he came home, it was usually just to change out his clothing or pick up something he'd left behind. He was angry that no-one was suing the store or the customers who stampeded through; he was haunted by the scene, the look of horror on the store employees' faces, the customers' looks of guilt, shock, heartache, and anger when the announcement came minutes later that the store was shutting, explaining that there were several injured, one fatally. "I've been standing on line since yesterday morning," one customer yelled out. It was the first time Johnny Allan had ever been tempted to strike a woman.

The next time we saw him, several weeks after Jean-David's death, he told me that Nikita and he had started using protection so they didn't accidentally bring a baby into a world as filthy as this one. He looked older, smelled like a pungent combination of cologne and weed, and his eyes had lost all of their exterior light, as if the pupils of his eyes had become enlarged, obscuring the deep browns of his iris. He cursed America, the almighty dollar, the supermarket chain he and Nikita had just quit, and Black Friday, which was creeping so close to Thanksgiving Thursday that even a second earlier and the two holidays would overlap like some kind of ugly bastard child of the past and present.

"What are you doing now," I said, "for money?"

"Nikita's parents are helping us out for a while we're looking for something else. We're going to live together," he said, without any of the earlier hint of excitement at the prospect of love or romance. It reminded me of my grandparents on my mother's side, who'd met during their expulsion from war-torn Prussia.

"But, whatever," he said. "It's not just the corporations or whatever. It's not even that surprising that people will stomp somebody down just to get a dollar DVD or a microwave. You think Guinea is a nasty place with fucking military motherfuckers in tanks bucking shots on the civilian population? What difference does it make what the cause of death is when in both cases people are dead because of other people's stupid priorities and egos?"

"You've gotta fight back," I said.

"I'm no fighter," he said.

"Stage a boycott."

"Of the store?"

"Or Black Friday," I said. "Or both. No-one protests anything in America anymore. It would take people by surprise."

"That's a good idea," he said, and I imagined for a moment that maybe *this* was Johnny Allan's calling, to become a leader, a community organiser, perhaps eventually a force in politics—"That's a *really* good idea," he repeated.

We hadn't seen Rachel in months—not since she broke up with Johnny—so that by the time we met for dinner one Friday evening in the West Village in a restaurant that specialised in haute cuisine and expensive French wine, we were talking for several moments about what had happened over the past weeks before she understood who it was we were speaking about.

"Who the fuck is Johnny?" she said.

"That's right," Amelia said, excitedly. "You'll know him as Allan."

"Oh, *him*. The *boy*," she said. "I never thought I'd become somebody's sugardaddy—"

"Sugar*mamma*, you mean?" Amelia said.

"He did something very confusing, in the beginning, when he offered to pay for dinner. He did confusing and contradictory things all the time. Maybe that's why you like him, Amelia, since you're always confusing and contradictory yourself. But this *mooch*, he'd bring his friends around and they eat and drink everything—my fucking éclairs, and the prosecco Giancarlo brought me from Venice—and, when I was out of town, he actually had people over to my place.

Finally I told him our time was up. He didn't seem upset or react at all. He actually seemed excited about it. He was just nodding with that smile on his face, like I'd just said something really kinky, or I was playing hard to get, and he was back the next day like nothing had happened. And we fucked because it's always better when you think you'll never see someone again, and this went on for another few weeks before I told him I meant it when I said it was time we see other people."

"You told him again that you wanted to see other people," Amelia said, snorting with laughter. "Except this time you clarified that that meant that the two of you were also finished."

"Yeah, he didn't seem to get it into his little brain the first time."

Amelia squealed with delight. "How am I confusing and contradictory?"

"You're a self-professed Luddite who works all day on a computer. You flirt constantly, with everyone, even old women, and you change your mind literally five times within a single conversation...Case closed."

Oh, Rachel...where have you been? She was quick, resolute and straightforward, the opposite of Amelia, who, it was true, was so indecisive at times that everything was always subject to change, and I had to assume that the evening plan would eventually turn into its opposite (if we planned to stay in and watch movies, for example, we'd end up at a bar until three a.m., flirting with the kitchen staff); this all changed when I realised I'd never eat again unless I was the one who made all of our plans, even though I was so laid-back that I would have been up for anything. This is the thing with spontaneity; like many personality traits, it comprises a spectrum, and too much of it, or too little, ultimately amount to being the same thing. Rachel, however, was another breed of human; she knew what she wanted down to the finest detail, always picked the restaurant, wine, appetizers, and even often ordered for Amelia.

"Have you ever been in an open relationship?" Amelia was asking Rachel...

"No," Rachel said. "They don't work. And who has the time?"

"Do *any* relationships really work?" Amelia said.

"You mean, except for ours," I said, on cue.

"Of course, our relationship is working right *now*, and it may work forever. But are the few failed open relationships we've heard about or seen in movies enough evidence to entirely dispel the genre? It's always exciting to think of what people are doing behind closed doors. If it wasn't for the Great

Depression, when the 20s disappeared overnight and the flappers lengthened their skirts and alcohol went for sale again, what do you think modern relationships would be like? After the First World War, only one out of ten girls in Britain were likely to settle down and get married and have a husband. The crash of the stock market set the clocks back, and it took fifty years before the next generation of flappers were back. All that social progress made in Harlem disappeared overnight, too…Let's go dancing," she said.

"I don't do dancing," Rachel said. "My hips don't move."

"You move your hips by moving your knees. It's a little-known, but true fact. You have to come with us."

We went to a place in the Lower East Side, in Alphabet City, just Amelia and I, where you could go to dance the Black Bottom and the Charleston and other 20s concoctions. We'd taken dance classes in London when we first started dating, and we were something of regulars there.

It was the next morning that I woke and walked across the house to the guest room where, looking out of the window at the street, I saw Johnny Allan's family unloading from the van, listening to the sound of their voices as they came up the steps speaking loudly in a mix of Fulani and French.

"I got fat," Binta said with a chuckle.

"How did that happen?" Aminata asked.

"Ramadan. It was right in the middle of summer this year."

"Did you bring your manioc sauce?" Aminata asked.

"I brought you scorpions and dust, darling."

I don't know if that's what they actually said, but it's fairly representative of how they spoke; it didn't take long, thanks to DNA supplied by my parents, I suppose, before I learned to understand, and even to speak Fulani, and the dust of Guinea (*dougou*) was a frequent topic of conversations for these Guineans, whose stories and cultural references were full of it—thanks to his mother's taunting, for years Johnny thought there was actually something called a dust sandwich.

But dust motes can live anywhere, and they were another of the many residents that shared our building, and were responsible for my unceasing hay fever.

The house was built in 1910. Amelia and I discovered this one day when we looked up the records online. *So that meant the 20s had lived here, too*, I overheard her thinking. It was funny to think of this old, rundown building housing the entire sweep of the 1920s, not just any one single part of it, but the entirety of it, thinking what characters had lived inside these walls, breathed the air wafting over from the street down there *still* there, how many renovations had occurred over the past century, different placements of furniture, how many bathtubs replaced (how many of them used for moonshine), how many bottles of wine uncorked, how many parties thrown by different people (in this city overflowing with immigrants), how many babies brought home from hospital, and how long had that TV inside the wood, sitting on the other side of the room, left over from previous tenants, been there? And the 20s would be here again, soon. By then, would *we* still be here? Would Johnny's family still live here? What will have changed—other than the soundtrack?

I hear the sound of his feet tromping up the steps, a bit of hesitation at the door and then the sound of the chime. He walks in, and I offer him, as is customary, a drink.

"I've got something I need to talk to you about…Yeah, sure..." he said, accepting the drink—Johnny was incapable of turning down anything free—"I'm not doing well. Nikita and me broke up, and well…this thing with Jean-David…I don't think I can go on for much longer. The fucking world is bullshit. I'm really…suicidal. I look around me, and all I see are hipsters and Zombies, and here I am at home and I'm sitting across from the dinner table from my guerrilla-warfare brother…I keep thinking about just disappearing, turning myself in and whatever. Not existing. I just feel like I was born into the wrong century."

"Go ahead, do it," I said. "Kill yourself."

9

It's strange to think of what tragedy accords the living. Only death is successful at conveying to us that we are alive. This is the thing with opposites, how they define one another. I'm happy about how my father went, in a cloud of dopamine and oxytocin, the original of a photograph of him and my mother in the Stuttgart daily in his hands (given to them by the photographer), hardened in place between index and middle fingers held across his chest, and next to it there a note I'd written him when I was five, "*Ich liebe dich, Vati*"—and next to it, my first translation: "I love you, Daddy." There was no suicide letter—should there have been? reduce life to *one* final statement, vouchsafe an explanation when none is needed?

Why cloud your life with redundant words when the actions speak so explicitly?

I understood why he killed himself—I even appreciated its overwhelming message of fidelity, of love. But to kill oneself for a cause is to live a life that encircles its narrowest limits, in disregard for its extensive and regenerative effects. And the result was that suddenly I was alone, the only child, with aunts and uncles none to whom I'd ever grown close, a number of friends—but these were contemporaries—and suddenly it was as if a clock that had been ticking quietly in the corner had stopped, and something essential to life, something like its coordinate axes, had been removed, and all that remained was silence. Abandonment, as if by God—God, moulded in the likeness of fathers; God, who had never existed to me—and so the death of my father meant that life had lost contact with its beginnings, its cosmic dust.

In the silence, pain. Time overspreading, overflowing hours with minutes that did not fit, erasing the barriers. My mother was dead, too, her ashes spread over the hillocks of her youth, in Bavaria…

There was no-one to speak to. The German post-post-war appetite for art and letters, restitution of Berlin as cultural paragon, its insatiable thirst for *geistige Dinge*, higher spiritual things and a life of the mind, meant that I had as much work as I required; by day, I traded in jingles and slogans and car ads: in German *auf Englisch* and back, in either direction; by night, I read German philosophy in their original and translated forms, by *them*, of course, listening for the sound in between the notes because this was the place where only I could hear them, an intangible landscape the three of us inhabited. It occurred to me much later that I'd been in love with them, and with my origins, and with the me that was an extension of them—not for their celebrity, or for their exploration of the ontological, but for the system of roots that tunnelled under-ground from seeds and stalks and peduncles, that kept me from ever having to contemplate reality other than in a search through the endless mazes of meaning that were all games, riddles, and corollaries, truly subsidiary to the roots that had grown through them, the life that had emerged nonetheless.

It's considered puerile to suffer prolonged heartbreak at the loss of one's parents. All can be overcome through psychology. The process of healing begins at once—with pain. The old and the dead become synonymous, and nostalgic beings are pitied for their inability to live fully in the present moment, clinging to what is gone. The path to happiness involves the release of these burdens, exfoliating the dead cells, looking ahead, living for oneself. But I found a woman who believed that the past was as alive as ever, under lock and key, awaiting someone to come and—thanks to the Berne convention and copyright laws—release it. And she didn't see my dead parents as dirty, or inviolate.

"You're starting to hear it in certain places, aren't you?" she said—to some she might have she sounded like a crazed lunatic—"*Midnight in Paris. Gatsby*...the 20s were unfinished, interrupted, a 'dream deferred...' "—so went her theory in its earliest sketches—"The past was cleared, always too quickly, to make room for the new. But that was dangerous. This is why we never really did heal ourselves. You erase progress, you erase development."

And here it was, for the very first time: "You're starting to hear it in certain places, and for the first time in the history of the planet, the greatest era of music—indeed, the first music of the modern era—is soon to be re-released, year by year, and if there is any hope for us as a species we'll listen because as important an era as the twenties were, we could probably stand to hear it twice."

"Tell me about the sound of your mother's voice," she said. "Describe it. How would you say that in German? Now translate it back. What are some of the expressions your father wore on his face? And your mother, how did she walk? Did they swear often? Did your father sound like *that* guy? What would they have thought of this Super President? How often do you reckon they got laid? How would your mum have reacted to that?..."

In the first few months of our relationship there wasn't a moment that went by in which she wasn't concerned with them, these people she'd never met; she'd somehow understood without articulating it how essential they were to me and how incredible her attention to this was for me.

The first great era of happiness in my own life after my parents' death came when I met Amelia. There was a waft of herbs (...basil, lavender...!) in the air, water had a taste, the crackle of records filled the soundtrack. It was the dead and gone that were magical because the moment the past ceases to exist, which is now...and now...and *now*!, everything restarts, rebuilt from what remains. After her mother's suicide, along with her father, the librarian, she began compiling lists of obsolete occupations; this led to other lists, and eventually one that included all of the songs from the 20s that, once released into the public domain, she would suggest for the movie soundtracks she was hired to put together. Retaining, cataloguing and preserving the past through its details helped me to replace wanton journeys between the lines of their texts; I reconstituted the past through its smells and grimaces, the occasional home video, their record collection, otherwise condemned to dust. My friends became Amelia's friends; at a nearby tavern on the high street, a regular gathering of disparate sorts came together and drank into the night, and we hosted many a dinner in our garden, creating the template for the parties we would later have in New York. It was through my parents' deaths that the seeds of my new family germinated, and with Amelia the past was always front and centre.

He studied my face for a long moment as I finished speaking, took a sip from his glass and then said. "So you're saying his suicide made you a better person?" The question was properly bereft of affability, and it was clear he understood exactly what I had been saying but had chosen not to acknowledge it. I was unaccustomed to a Johnny whose constant excitement, at the smallest details of life, had been substituted by a caustic indifference—indifference, his generation's curse, but *not* Johnny's...: "So if I kill myself I might be improving the lives of others around me?" he said, with a slight chuckle.

I stared back at him coldly, "You haven't understood a single word I've said."

"You're trying to teach me some kind of lesson," he said, again rather lukewarmly.

"Allan," I said. "If you kill yourself, you won't be around to regret it. Jean-David is dead, unnecessarily. Tell *him* what you're thinking of doing."

The Thursday before Thanksgiving had been the last of our weekly pizza dinners with Johnny Allan. Now booted from Nikita's, he was back at home, though we didn't see much of him. More often, we *heard* him (his voice was instantly recognizable through its pauses, the reliance on his lower register, the way in which it rose and fell within its actually rather small range…); we overheard yelling, the treble of his mother's voice, then his baritone. Sometimes he still didn't come home for a few days. But when he was there, it was as if the walls shook; even though there was a constant sound of running and giggles and high-pitched squeals from the children, Amelia constantly pointed out that there was a tonal distinction between the times that he was home and the times when he was not; this was the reason why the sound production team on a film recorded several seconds of noise when everyone was gathered—every room has a natural tone, influenced by the bodies in it—and who was I to argue with her ear?

In the mornings I woke and put on the kettle still in the dark. The whistling, the noise from the bedroom: *Alan*! We sat next to each other on the green couch. We still had plenty to say to one another. Then—the 7-train, and the faces of the half-dead, of the half-living, of Zombies and Selfies (but also of really fit girls in coats, in black-rimmed glasses: unaware, unfazed by the disbelieving ogles of men and women), everyone with something in front of them (tablets, books, phones…); I re-read Kafka, Melville, and Joyce (recognizing, for the first time, the child in "Araby" for the stalker that he now was), standing, watching who got on and off at each stop, exiting at Grand Central, into the snow and the chill through the embassy-laden streets, out of the United States, into the United Nations, into my office, divided from the General Assembly by a glass partition, united by a pair of headphones.

I thought about quitting. (There is joy in quitting.) I'd been at the UN for three years now, and I couldn't stand walking on the same side of the street every day to work, taking the same path, boarding any kind of train and taking it the same number of stops, going through the security detail at work, repeating the same platitudes to the same people in similar dress…It was for this reason that there was nothing more intolerable to me than delays that lengthened the time of these redundant journeys; in those moments, I felt as if my life were being overridden by the banal. Quitting and routine, forever like Mercury on course or in retro-; a mercurial comportment meant that you lived life in flight, enchained to a sort of restlessness; the thought of losing any of my rituals filled me with dread and, at the end of the day, *everything* in reverse, but now the wrinkles (in clothing, faces…), and there are many ways a tie can be undone; sometimes I saw the same faces, as oblivious to me in the evening as in the morning (occasionally, there were nods, sudden, panicky, reflexive smiles or half-greetings, people interrupted from their dazes, having internalised my face from before, thinking that I knew them and then, conjoined with the look of familiarity I gave then, confused me with someone other than a stranger looking at them for just too long (a weirdo…a stalker)—by now I knew something about them, by the things they carried, the change in dress from day-to-day, in the way they wore their hair…Summer, despite the relentless American air con, undid everyone by the afternoon, and I loved the winter, the preserved freshness, bodies in refrigeration, all of the molecules held close together. Everything was on ice; only time, of all things, continued on at the same invariable gait. Time and tea—everything else was mutable.

I walked into the apartment; the door to the studio was always closed. For her birthday, I'd installed an LED studio warning light over the door that said "ON AIR—RECORDING" (a hipster extravagance if ever there was one);

when I arrived home, the lights were flashing with great ceremony. But she knew what time I'd be home and, unless she was so deeply engrossed in what she was doing to the point that only her bladder knew the score (and my first glimpse of her would be of her running down the hallway to the bathroom), she'd emerge around seven, often in the same outfit she'd been wearing when I left in the morning (pyjamas, mostly), to ask me what had happened during the day, and to share dramatic tales of her day inside: conversations had with ADs or boom operators and other members of her various teams, with the postmen (who adored her); or with Gang Lu, the charming Chinese restaurant owner who asked her for $100 every time she ordered food and then when she went to collect it told her he'd already delivered it to the New Jersey Turnpike.

I liked the way she talked *about* our conversations, how she would say "Today you had more stories than I did," or "My stories were really better than yours" or "You're not in top form today," or "That story is the most badass one," or "That would have been funnier had you emphasised the guy's grandmother more" or "Now how would *I* have told that story?"

"And news from the second floor, sightings, etc.?" I'd say, at some point.

"Slow day," she'd say. Or: "Saw Aminata, who showed me some of her brilliant photos." Or: "I saw him from the window, walking down the street with Souleymane."

We didn't like this much. Souleymane was serious and seemed to read something converse into anything you said. Laughter never tempted him. What he saw, and what he'd seen, was somehow better because it was terrible, and seeing the terrible was preferable because it meant you were living in the real world. In Conakry, he had a driver and a job in the government, and he lived in a nice house in a neighbourhood with generators and, if Johnny was serious about his aversion to technology, then Conakry was his place. It was violent, but it was *good* violence, the kind a man should not be afraid of, not as bad as what was portrayed on television, and you could see the violence, whereas in America it was invisible, happened behind closed doors, outsourced to off-site torture centres in foreign countries like his; and had Johnny ever been with a girl from Guinea, light, dark or in-between? In Guinea the man is respected, he takes more than one wife, and the children are raised by the community, not by contracted strangers. (These were nearly the same list of reasons why Aminata, who listened to them talking, and had passed the details on to us, had chosen to leave.)

"Then why don't you have a second wife?" Johnny said.

"Have you seen my first one?" Souleymane replied. She was beautiful, but not personable, but his point was evident. "Anyway, in my case, if I took a second wife, the first one would never talk to me again."

"Isn't it dirtier than here?" Johnny asked, pulling the sanitizer out of his pocket and offering some to his brother.

"If you ever get tired of the dust, we can go to les îles de Loos by pirogue. It's more beautiful than you have seen, and it's in *la Guinée*, only an hour away from Conakry. You can die anywhere, as you now know."

"I'm dead already," Johnny said. "It's just not official yet."

He was ill—he'd come down with some kind of flu, nothing too fancy or severe, but enough to knock him off his feet for a few days and render him null; I came by one late evening when he was well enough to welcome a visitor.

"Feeling better?" I said.

"Not exactly."

"How's your *mental* health?"

"My mom bought me a one-way ticket to Conakry this morning," he said. "She thinks I'm in bad shape or whatever."

"She bought you a ticket to Guinea *without asking you?"* I couldn't believe what I was hearing.

"Yeah. It was going to get crowded around here anyway, now that Souleymane's son is staying to go to school—they want him to learn English. There's no way I'd share a room with a kid anyway. I'm 23 years old, man."

"You'll have your own room in Conakry?"

"Yeah."

"Do you *want* to go there?"

"It doesn't matter to me, man. My mom—all she does is cry dramatically and say that she can't stand missing out on my life. She keeps talking about all the money she spent on this one-way ticket. And there's some females she wants to introduce to me."

"You'd let your mother set you up?"

"Why not?" he said. "She said I wouldn't have to marry them or anything."

"What does your dad say about all of this?"

"He doesn't know."

"He doesn't know? Don't you think he'll be upset?"

"You know we don't get along."

"And why *is* that?"

"We see things from a different point of view. He believes that life is all about work, with no play. The only activity we have to do together is to watch TV...We don't have the connection you and your father had, like we're into the same kinds of things. What's the point of doing the kind of meaningless work he does?"

"But is that a reason to run away from here? Aren't you afraid of the violence? Battles between various ethnic groups?"

"It's not as bad as you might think."

"You'll know better than I."

"I gotta get out of here, Alan. I don't want to go to Guinea, but my mom bought me a ticket…I gotta get outta this bridge-and-tunnel Zombieland before I—what's that thing you're always saying—become redundant; with new spots opening up right and left and people like y'all showing up from London and whatever, and so much change, it's easy to forget you're standing in the same place. And what does it matter if I die in Conakry when I was going to die here?"

"But—"

"What I keep thinking about, more than anything is what you told me. You guys are my mentors and, well, the moment I knew I needed to go was when I thought about what you said about me mastering French and Fulani. About how foreign languages were as good as degrees. And it was the first time in a while that I felt anything besides anger or disappointment, or nothing at all, since Jean-David's murder. And then I thought about something that Souleymane said to me, too, about how there was probably no place on earth more behind on technology than Guinea. I took it as a sign from the universe. That's all there is to it."

"If you think *Queens* is dirty—" I began.

"It's a dirty motherfucking world."

10

Once the decision had been made, Johnny Allan's departure from New York dragged on for weeks—Binta's holiday had yet to conclude, and for what seemed an interminable amount of time, the Diallo extended nuclear family remained, filling up the days with the architecture of a family visit, which involved multiple people waiting in bay for everyone else to arrive, then slow, incremental movements from apartment to door to stairway landing, to the next door, to the street and so on, forward and reverse, over days.

In Aminata's photography from these January and February days, there's a lot to see: we find Binta in the kitchen, her lips pursed in concentration, an expression of consternation extending her forehead, the camera catching from an angle a trace of her suspicious eyes; Souleymane and Johnny are sat on the stoop next to a parked bicycle frozen to the railing, Souleymane miming gregarious, the smile here one that is simultaneously drawing apart his lips, yet against some considerable unseen resistance, while Johnny in his obliviousness to the camera looks straight into it in a way that the first message conveyed from the expression is that in the photo he is alive, he is a person, and whose second message is a lack of self-consciousness or ego, that if you came upon him at this moment, you would identify him as the same man in the photo—Johnny is wearing a pastel shirt with flowers, open slightly, even with the ice and frozen steps beside him, even while wearing a jacket, bearing his hairless chest. There is a photo of Johnny lifting his niece; another is of Denis standing in front of the door on the inside of the flat smiling awkwardly. There is another of Johnny's niece alone; the smile is so large it causes a ripple in her cheek that looks on her oily, elastic skin like the indistinct ridge in a ball of dough. There is Souleymane's wife, walking hesitantly through Jackson Heights, the portrait of the distant beauty whose price for her delicate, avian face is estrangement from life; even the positioning of her feet betray her discomfort with her environment, the heavy winter jacket over the kaftan only the final coat of paint on a photo whose colours leak through the drying ink. The only photo that features Aminata was taken in the bathroom with Binta; Aminata is holding the camera six or seven centimetres away from her face, so we catch everything but the edge of her face in her reflection in the mirror. It seems clearly to be the expression of an observer, and of a photographer thinking of the room in her own, particular, camera-shaped dimensions, looking over at her subject intrigued by what she might capture, her lips slightly twisted in indifference to this particular photo's potential for singularity, and thus Binta is reduced to her actions, to the gaze that includes her face, her thoughts, the length of her forehead extended by consternation. The best photos are all of the children, and of Johnny, who in each incarnation looks so much like himself that it's easy to imagine the other two dimensions are somehow enfolded into, or accounted for by, the first. Was it this lack of self-consciousness and ego that allowed him to be so supremely himself, and was it *this* that gave us this premonition of greatness (still unchanneled into greatness), or was it that, unlike his generation—the first in the history of the planet to fully merge self-documentation and experience, whose cameras faced in both directions, and who, through archiving, deleting, pruning, never diverting attention, had decided they in fact preferred life flat to round—Johnny was oblivious to the camera and its representation of himself, whether because he really did not care or notice or understand or value the permanence of the photo or the memory of minds that carry impressions through a lifetime, or because perhaps the pervasiveness of this documentation had caused him to always be the person we are when no-one is looking?

Aminata's photos, which were evolving at a spectacular rate, show the family standing in front of the cinema, the children playing with the cats, Souleymane standing at the subway station with all of his bags to head to the airport on 15 January, the children in the snow (and Janell's snow angel) and a nice series of photos of Binta and Souleymane's wife carefully choosing vegetables and fruit at the local grocer. There were also several photos she took of me and several of Amelia, mostly in our apartment, several in the bedroom, that were among her most daring.

In the newspapers online, I continued to read about struggles in Conakry: trenchant articles about government corruption, forced marriages, rape, exploited resources, the absence of schools, hospitals where it wasn't uncommon to go in with one disease and come out with several more, protests and strikes where people were gunned down or struck or imprisoned, widespread poverty, soaring food prices, killings, lynchings, people set on fire, shootings and beheadings often to do with ethnic and religious clashes, lack of electricity, where students study in the light of petrol stations or storefronts, suppression of freedom of the press, soldiers attacking radio stations, and so on. I kept thinking, if he goes, he won't be back for years, not with the fortune his mother must have spent on the tickets and when they only come to the States every three or four years. They had some money, but international flights were major investments these days, and what would he do there to make money?

But then what excuse would he have *not* to go…? If only he had music, art, education, *any* kind of passion…—I was reminded of soldiers drafted to war because they were young men without commitments. Here, it wasn't a question of whether Johnny had greatness in him; he *needed* it.

I felt responsible. I'd said that languages were as good as diplomas (or better). And I think Amelia and I had been pushing him, whether aware of it or not, to make a choice, a radical one.

With Amelia in New Orleans for a few weeks as sound recordist on another jazz documentary, I took it upon myself to attempt to undo the damage and give Johnny Allan every reason I could not to leave New York (while also escaping some of my own monotonous routines…which, to a certain degree, were also among my favourite moments of living).

Amelia, who wouldn't return until a few days before Johnny's departure, volunteered her "Sucking the Life out of New York" list, which was her catalogue of places to take visitors from out of town, a list of places unknown to the local citizen for whom New York is a city created in his or her own likeness. At the Levee, Johnny had made the announcement to his friends at the New Year's Party, and so now he didn't go anywhere without Algernon and Samuel (whose girlfriend had just given birth to a son), who were just as upset and sad as we were that Johnny was going and didn't want to miss a minute of his final days in New York.

Johnny kept his usual slot at the Levee, and on the nights on which I was too knackered from work and the late-nights to coax myself into movement, he saw Samuel and Algernon alone. The rest of the time it was the four of us, Algernon covered in chains and tattoos that coiled around his neck, his head inside his love poems (all about his petulant Polish pet), his incessant talk of DJ gear ("I know you're a head, Alan," he'd say to me, "Son, I was in Camden back in the day, and niggers had their shit so pimped out, I got all dizzy and tearful just looking at them sick-ass Stanton and Numark tables"); Samuel with his shaved head and constant talk of people he'd messed up for saying shit he didn't like; I got to where I liked them quite a bit, for their loyalty to Johnny, their open-mindedness and thrill and willingness to participate in the rituals at places like the Nuyorican Poet's Café in Alphabet City, where we went for a slam, where they stood and cheered and shouted out responses to the poets and hosts, chiming in when prompted, encouraging the poet when fumbling a line—"You got it, son"—, snapping their fingers, going along with the game. The Shanghai Mermaid hosted a special "secret" underground 20s India event about which Amelia refused to speak to me she was so upset she wouldn't be able to attend (yet told me she would divorce me if I didn't); my office mate Pramit lent the four of us kurtas, long robes in multi-colours that weren't so different from the grand boubous of West Africa, and we found ourselves in a hotel-size palace of rooms among hundreds of faux Indians and Britons from the colonial period (and others who just dressed vaguely 1920s) in costume, listening to music from Punjab and 20s jazz, watching the women (not Indian) dancing as if they were. A woman swinging from cloth strung from pillars danced with a snake in the middle of the room, and Johnny en route to the bathroom ended up sharing a cigarette with her in the rain under an umbrella, when she told him that she included the snake in all of her bedroom affairs. A Brazilian friend of mine from the embassy was playing bossa nova in the Village; upon Samuel's request (he'd fallen in love with the conceit of playing tourist in his own city), we went to a strip club in Astoria where, to the dismay of his new girlfriend from Pennsylvania, the mostly Eastern European girls (whom Algernon incessantly contrasted with his girlfriend throughout the night, saying she was much prettier and had a much better body, with perkier curves) never stripped beyond their underwear; and we went on a tour given by a high-end real-estate agency for rich customers in the market for expensive short-term furnished apartment rentals (to make it even more fun for us, we decided to have Samuel pose as a hip hop star and us as his entourage—Johnny and I wore suits and played his business managers, while Algernon pretended to be his lover, and we swore the agents to secrecy, explaining that it would kill his career if anyone were to find out he was gay).

Things were going according to plan, until one late night, Samuel, Johnny and a number of other friends—of ours, of theirs—had come back to my place, and I'd decided to make some dough for pizzas and a vat of mojitos (that only tasted vaguely *of* mojito), when Johnny, helping pound what mint remained from the Hanging Gardens, told me about how happy he was to be leaving New York in just a matter of days and going to Guinea and that he was eager to be heading away from this New York of hipsters and cellphonies to disappear into a place that didn't pretend the rest of the world didn't exist. I told him, now that the hours were running down, and because I'd become drunk sampling the mojito trying to make it taste like mojito, that I didn't think he should go and, more than that, I felt it was an incredibly stupid idea that showed how little he knew about the world, that further reflected how little he'd read and his ignorance of the world beyond New York. I told him he was a fully grown child and couldn't mooch off his family and friends forever.

"Why do you think I want to leave New York?" he said. "Thanks for the reality check, Alan. Man, I understand what going to Guinea is like. I know how dangerous it is. I used to live there, remember, when I was a kid. But I can't believe *you* just said all of this. Obviously, I'm not as smart as you. I don't know all of this shit. And now it's my turn to call you out on this: you're contradicting yourself. How else the fuck am I going to learn what life is like if I don't see the danger, experience it all? That's the thing with opposites, right—how they define one another. That's what you said." Tears poured out of his eyes.

"Shit," I said. "I'm really sorry." But the damage had been done.

"It's okay," he said. "You're right. I'm sorry, man. I—anyway now I know how you really see me. And, well—it's cool. I'm sorry. You know, I really do love you. You're one of the best things that's ever happened to me.

"I love you, too," I said. "That's the only reason why I'm worried about you going to Guinea."

He stood there for a long time, saying nothing. Then, he changed the subject…"I want to ask you about something else," he said, pausing, eyeing me carefully, almost, for an instant, accusatorily.

"You took naked photos for my aunt?"

"Yeah, I…Aminata asked me if I would." I said. I felt a surge of heat flush my face. "I'm European. We don't think of the human body as taboo," I said, again rather pedantically.

"Sometimes I feel like Europe has it all together, and this is the most backward place."

"No," I said. "Europe is past its prime. Now we just want to sit around judging the rest of the world."

"With sex, you're definitely freer."

"I don't even know about that," I said. "Maybe."

The first of several misunderstandings was afoot, and this conversation would play a role in this, and was only the first of several such instances of contradictions, misunderstandings or coincidences (or outright subterfuge) that would change our lives and lead me toward the end of this narrative. The next one would have to do with Johnny's exit from New York.

Surprisingly, when Binta told Denis that she had bought Johnny a ticket, Denis turned and, nonchalantly, asked Johnny if he wanted to go to Guinea. Johnny explained that Guinea was his heritage and that it was time he met some distant cousins and aunts and uncles (his mother was constantly filling Johnny with new reasons to leave New York, even though the truth was, I later realised, that the choice had been made for Johnny, on his behalf, and *that* was in fact its greatest allure). His father said, simply, "That's fine," and left the room, under the influence of no apparent distress or disappointment.

His nephew, Allan (Souleymane's son), ever since eating a hot dog at Times Square, had had recurrent stomach aches that had kept him from participating in family outings and instead he was positioned in front of a TV in Johnny's bedroom, where he spent the first several weeks of his newfound American life watching cartoons and Disney films without subtitles in French; he was on his second cold, which the New York chill only exacerbated (Conakry's wintry temperatures very rarely dipped below 20°C); it was not uncommon for visitors to get sick adjusting to the processed food and portions and preservatives and food-like food. With 72 hours remaining in America, Johnny became suddenly aware that his life in New York was over, that his rituals—what he, like me, had found to be the bane of his existence—would be among the first things to come loose, that when he came back Algernon and Samuel would likely be married, Janell would be as unrecognizable to him as she was to her mother, his interior ecosystem would be swimming with the waters of the locals Guinean wells and he'd return another man (in his mid- or late- twenties perhaps), if ever he did return. Before, he had drawn enthusiasm from the notion of himself the weary traveller returned, refined, his posture erect, carrying the dust of the exotic in his pockets like sand from the beach. Now, some of my warnings had finally caused him to contemplate the opposite.

With 60 hours remaining, Amelia came home from New Orleans, with stories of Southern conviviality and hospitality, and a profound desire that, as soon as I could, I go with her there—where the dust of its golden age was settling into a veneer of swaggerish ruin, and the storms of the past had created more jobs than any government initiative ever could, and the evenings were full of streetcars and jazz bars and the atmosphere of a carnival. And she'd met all kinds of personalities, real American types, with slow, fascinating accents, folks who told stories: fishermen and poets and street performers and restaurateurs and the denizens of a burgeoning film industry that called to mind the Los Angeles of the 20s.

I caught her up on the past few weeks: our outings, the night of mojitos, Johnny's reaction to Aminata's photos ("How strange," she said), the young Allan's recumbent convalescence and Johnny's rising doubts. And that's when it dawned on her:

"Why doesn't *Allan* fly back on Johnny's ticket?" she said, jazzed by the idea. "Do they have the same surname? They *must*."

And, just as quickly, she was struck again by epiphany:

"My God! Johnny returning to Guinea was the plan from the start," she said. "He's not on a one-way ticket at all, is he? He's taking his nephew's return flight back. This has nothing to do with his mother's concerns about his mental health."

"You're right!" I exclaimed, recognizing the truth.

We explained her discovery to Johnny who, to our surprise, was unimpressed.

"Yeah, that's probably true. But Allan's staying here. That's what Souleymane wants. So it doesn't even matter."

"But you don't have to go to Guinea," Amelia said. "If the ticket is for the return journey, then it's not like your mum shelled out a thousand dollars for you on a one-way ticket. You'll merely be wasting the return, which would probably only be worth a couple hundred dollars."

"But we can't waste the ticket, or anything. She would be really upset. That's just not compatible with how Guineans think. In Guinean culture, every scrap of paper or food or metal is worth something."

When we told Aminata about our discovery, she was convinced we were right, and began immediately shaking her head: "Binta has been involved in this kind of mischief since the day she was born," she said. "She's a master of deception and getting her way."

And Johnny would spend the next several years under her manipulative care. Amelia and I were beginning to feel rather desperate.

The only thing the young Allan seemed interested in eating was manioc leaf sauce and foods cooked from fresh ingredients. Janell hovered over him eating cheese puffs as he watched *Peter Rabbit.*

With 42 hours remaining, we all met at the Levee for Johnny Allan's last office hour; in tow were some of Johnny's closest friends, Aminata, Samuel and Algernon of course, the Polish girl, and even some of our friends we were surprised to find there, whom Johnny had invited one by one over the telephone, asking them rather imperiously to carefully copy down the time and address, in his rendition of a retro invite à la the 1990s. The NYU girl, Trisha, whom we'd nearly forgotten and whom most of us had never met, turned up and was treated like she'd been around since the beginning, and was offered kindnesses and shows of semi-condolence as if she were Johnny's recognized and true long-lost soulmate.

The time passing as it does in the last 24 hours of a condemned man's life, there was even time for killing time, for ritual, to fit in conversations on the stoop and in our flat smoking my pipe and Johnny his rollies, until, at just past noon, Denis Toussaint returned home six hours premature to announce that he had just been to the doctor and had been told his heart was in a bad state, an artery was clogged and if he didn't get the situation under control immediately, he would be dead before summer.

Before the hour was up, Johnny said to his mother, "I can't leave him alone," and she said nothing, which was the same thing as agreeing, or capitulating, and before the end of the day, the other Allan, Souleyman's son, boarded the Royal Air Maroc flight back home with Binta, his mother and sister, because he'd never adapted to America food anyway and, as Johnny had said to me just a few days before, Guineans were anything but wasteful.

11

Here it is, the whole story, with every bloody detail. The Diallo family had parted, and here was Johnny Allan standing on the stoop, holding a cigarette. He was contemplative, and had mixed feelings about what had just happened. His shoulders had visibly dropped, but he stared off into the distance as if there was nothing there. He felt like he'd been left behind and would never get out of New York. We reassured him, explaining that it wasn't meant to be, repeating to him our best logic, that it was a dangerous time to be in Guinea, and the universe had bigger plans for him—Amelia was certain of this, that greatness was just around the corner, not just for him, but for everyone—and that he just needed to be patient, he'd find his way, and we'd be here to help. Amelia said that she would teach him how to work with sound. "Sound is everything," she said. "I realised this the first time I was laying down the score over a tense, emotional scene in a film. A light, upbeat tune can turn death into comedy; tempo affects tempo, and there is nothing more intoxicating than hearing all of these sounds in isolation, then tweaking them to endless effect." He seemed intrigued by this.

They began their sessions immediately:

"Look at this," she said, and pressed play—the sound was delayed by a half-second, meaning that mouths were moving with no words, like in dubbed martial arts movies from the 70s and 80s; the sound of cars crashing came seconds after the cars had already collided. "Reality is already synced," Professor Amelia began: "A door makes a sound when it closes. A bus blazes down the street on cue. Even the slightest sound, of a cat's feet thumping on the floor or a hand waved in someone's face, happens with no delay, simultaneous with the action. But, every once in a while, things seem off—you see people are talking but you don't hear any sound at all, or there's static, or interference. The glass breaks. The shattering sound comes too late, so no-one knows to get out of the way. You start to think you live in a world where everything is just a little bit off, where the business of living and life and human existence is fractured. It can all be corrected through editing. You can remove sounds you don't like or turn the volume down. You can lay a soundtrack over the prosaic and turn it into something else." She overlaid *Mojo Hand Blues* by Ida Cox upon a scene where a young man in his 20s is simply walking down the street. On screen, the camera shifted from mid-range to close-up shots, and then to a wide-screen angle of a man walking, a neutral expression on his slightly bearded face.

Within a week, Johnny got a job at a small pizzeria in Bushwick that both sold full pies and pizza by the slice; this new post delighted us. After a few weeks, he could spin the dough on the ends of his fingers like a basketball. Very quickly, he cultivated a new look; his hair had grown longer, and he wore a goatee and let his sideburns hang down slightly, a few millimetres down; even in trendy Brooklyn, he stood out. On the first day, he fell in love with the girl from Albania who handled the orders and worked the phones—she was beautiful but wore too much makeup, we thought, and they were very quickly in the throes of newfound love.

"We have these conversations that take place over hours," Johnny said, "She'll say something to me and then the phone'll ring and she'll be busy for the next fifteen minutes, and then I'll say something to her, and we'll talk for a little while, and then I'm dealing with customers and taking their money—

people are coming in and the boss is on us and I'm rolling the dough, but in between we're having these conversations about love and sex and life and then we leave together and go back to her place in East New York with her brother and sister and their dog, and she and I go back to her bedroom and we continue the conversations until the morning and then we sleep until the afternoon and then get ready for work."

He came over regularly, but rarely for dinner, and would work with Amelia, or watch Amelia work for hours, sometimes half the night, their faces swimming in computer light. They would talk, too, and the next morning, on the green couch, in the imaginary light of the broken television, she'd give me the highlights ("He said something that had me in a fit—oh, that he wanted to tattoo *our* names on his arms, next to his ex-wife's"), always seeing him, through his inexhaustible innocence that made him like a child for whom any sophistication is greeted as precocity, even as he got older and his face grew more chiselled, more full, more bearded. Were we seeing a glimpse of his future? Is *this* what he would become? A pizzaiola? A chef? A baker? Or would he work with sound, like Amelia? Would he work in the movies? (And why not, I always thought, front and centre on screen? The camera loved him.)

She found herself attracted to him, she always had been to some extent, but it had burgeoned over time—*he's the kind of guy that people root for unequivocally, who you just want things to work out for*, Amelia had said more than once when we revisited the question of his potential for greatness (finally coming into view?)—but her attraction to him was separate from this. It wasn't a feeling of safety, nor even of lust. Not the look in his eyes. Not his ears, more finely tuned that hers, she said—the ears of an owl or a dolphin or a wax moth…Nor the look, nor the *reality of that look* (how he grew a moustache not just to grow a moustache or to see himself with a moustache or because you're *supposed* to grow a moustache, but because it began to grow on his face on its own and he liked it…) Not his clever or original insights, born of his unique life experiences, his unbiographical story, incompatible with biographies we've all read and recognise and that feel so familiar to us we could fill in the blanks on our own, nor his emergence on the face of this earth a fully grown, 23-year-old baby, who spoke three languages the three stages of history, one of the tribe, of the nomads of the Sahara; the other of the colonisers and world sophisticates and the bourgeois bohème; the other the lingua franca, the language of money and the Zeitgeist, each offering him a different identity without his ever having to leave home. Not the fact that he was her partner in crime in technophobia, herself in male form—nor even all of these things together. What, *then*? Sometimes the world does not offer you reasons, but you feel something in your gut so profoundly it's as if that feeling had been there since you the day you were born. Amelia wasn't in love with Johnny Allan—it wasn't *that*. It was a much more animalistic or chemical feeling, an urge that was growing and growing and, by not being consummated, had no other choice but to swell up more. (And didn't I, who felt the same way about Rachel, understand that?)

I left for a conference in Berlin focusing on Gestalt psychology, and specifically its rendering into other languages. I was invited by some intimate friends of my parents whom I'd known as a child, and who were keen on including me in the conference so that I might introduce some of their work and so that we might all come together again and speak of them and of the past. I flew via London and spent three days with friends and family, and I dropped in on our storage facility in Hounslow, a few miles from the airport, where I was to gather up some of our things and ship them to Queens, now that we had chosen it as our permanent abode.

In the meantime, Johnny Allan made love to Mimoza Mecini while her brothers played loud, violent video games in the room next door, and the dog barked every time it heard the sound of their kissing. Johnny went to work, suggesting to his boss new toppings: arugula, clams and bacon, fresh parsley…but was told that they would just stick with what was already working, in the background the same radio station recycling popular Top 100 anthems that all sounded like the same song, the same artist (music for children, Amelia called it...). And, on alternate nights, when he went home to look in on his father (who was back at work, who'd been prescribed medication to reduce his cholesterol), he turned up chez nous smelling of dough, and Amelia made them both salads (of arugula, of fresh parsley…), and they watched silent films on the projector, toasting the 20s, the best decade that had ever been.

One night he left our apartment at three a.m., after having spent the evening talking rather heatedly about politics (or was it that Amelia had, and Johnny had mostly listened?), after Johnny had said that he did not believe in government and institutions, after which Amelia said that she believed that no-one his age did, that this was the beauty of his anarchic generation and another reason why they would be the next great age: their irreverence for the old institutions, their intolerance of government, polarity, affirmative action, their hypertolerance of the Other, their hyper political correctness, their hypercategorising of people, their hypernostalgia and free love and open relationships (all while maintaining an appearance of hyperindifference)…"We all hate hipsters, but no-one knows what a hipster is. Anti-conformist conformists? Meta-humans? The loosely defined category is so loose as to include anyone: certainly it can't be that just because you grow facial hair or like your food grown locally, or cycle to work, or care to dress like you don't care that you're a hipster. If that's the case, then we're all becoming hipsters and it's not a counterculture—it's *culture*—and the people we see as epitomising hipsterism are just the most exaggerated or the most vocal or the most obscene among us. Everyone is hipster-like, because hipsterism represents our most updated tendencies. What makes a hipster a hipster is that he does things not because he likes them but because he thinks it will be interesting or make him more interesting. The whole point of the trip is to record it, not to live it, because life is something ironic, a parody of itself. That's what the hipster has in common with the blogger and the social networking addict and the Zombie. In his heart, the hipster takes nothing seriously, other than his fear of death, and sees everything as ironic, even himself as a canvas for expression. He can't take anything seriously that takes itself too seriously, which is why government, religion, relationships, and all of the other institutions of life have lost their force to him. And he takes himself too seriously as a point of irony. What makes you different, Johnny, is that you don't take yourself seriously even just a little bit..."

What did Johnny say to this? He listened, and he thought about what she was saying, and he wondered what made him different even though he felt he possessed so many characteristics that were just like those of everyone else. Was he *really* different? Was there something special about *him*, of all people? Was it that he was incapable of seeing himself in context? How would Gestalt psychology define *his* self-organizing tendencies—would they be deemed different from the norm, the ordinary?

When he left the apartment, she was looking at him, watching his body—the sum of its parts, but not greater than them—move across the floor, every sound perfectly synched as he strode to the door, walked out, shut it and stood there for several moments just outside, wondering if what he felt was real, and what it meant. He went home and took a long shower that drained the building of its hot water and then a half-hour later returned to our door and knocked. She came to answer it quickly enough, but by then he was already gone. But she knew it had been him, his knock. She went back into the apartment, and it occurred to her that he was just one floor below but there was no way she could communicate with him, and this was a tremendous turn-on, what bound them together, that she *couldn't* reach him through any of the normal channels.

She opened the window in our bedroom and slipped out onto the fire escape, where she felt the cold penetrate her pants in direct contact with her skin. She crept down step by step, until she was in front of his bedroom and, at an angle through the blinds, she saw him in the room, shirtless, his feet in the air, his forearms on the ground. She shivered; he dropped to the floor, picked up a book, lay down on the floor with it…She tapped on the glass, and then he opened the window and looked out at her in surprise and let her in.

Who pulled the other into embrace, where warm flesh met frigid, defrosting skin, beginning their slow fusing to a single temperature? Johnny didn't remember.

"Is this okay?" he asked.

"It was inevitable," Amelia said.

When I returned from Europe, Amelia was alone in the sound studio, the LED light on. I broke custom and knocked. She opened and threw her arms around me. "My dear!" she said, and then followed me into the living room, where I began pulling out knick-knacks from the trip and items from our separable pasts: a lamp made of mosaic tiles a friend had brought me back from India, a multi-coloured vase with a chicken on it, a tortilla press my parents had brought me back from a conference in Mexico, some books and records, one of Amelia's jewellery boxes…And there were more to come; some items I'd shipped, and they would arrive by post over the next several days.

I couldn't have been happier to have returned. The New York through the window of the airplane had looked like an antique city made of the mosaic tiles of the lamp, and the thought of returning to our apartment and our life in Queens filled me with joy, a feeling of total satisfaction, as if perhaps I had gotten things in my life perfectly right.

Johnny came round that evening; he seemed apprehensive, something that, when I asked him about it, the tumbler in his hands, the bourbon slinking down his throat, he attributed to his job, to his status as a man on an assembly line, reproducing the same pizza over and over again, with the same ingredients, to the same redundant soundtrack: "He won't play jazz. All I want is twenty minutes of Duke Ellington every day. I might as well still be working at that other store…you know, the one whose name I'll never pronounce again. Alan, it's the same day over and over again."

I was shocked to hear him say this; making a pizza to me was a poetic act, how the fresh starter built itself from the air, how it lived and changed with the temperature of a room, the weather…This statement put a serious dint in my plans for his becoming one of the great pizzaioli…"And what about…God, what's her name?" I began. "It's hard to keep them straight now," I said with a smile.

"Mimoza," he said. "There's not *that* many of them."

"Right. The drink!" Amelia said.

"Huh?" he said.

Amelia burst out laughing. "You've never heard of a mimosa? In this city of brunch…" She was in hysterics.

Johnny laughed uncomfortably.

"You should invite her over Thursday," I said. I was thinking that maybe the past several weeks had erased Johnny's memories of our times making pizza together.

"When did you get back?" Denis Toussaint said when I saw him the next day.

"Just yesterday," I said.

"Yes, I saw you arriving, from the window," he said.

"Then you *already* know when I got back," I said. It was incredible, I thought, the American capacity for stating the obvious.

"I was surprised to see you," he said. "I didn't realize you were gone."

"Sorry I didn't think to let you know," I said. Was this an American landlord thing; should I have advised him of my international trip? His forehead furrowed, an expression I'd never seen on his face before.

"And how is your health?" I said.

"I'm feeling much better," he said. And then he looked at me carefully before speaking, and then said, "Alan, I don't think your wife has been alone."

"What do you mean?"

"Exactly what it sounds like I mean," he said.

"Certainly Johnny has been there," I said. "And sometimes she meets people she works with, and friends."

"I would say Amelia has been having an affair," he said.

"With whom?"

"I don't know," he said.

"What *do* you know?" I said. "That's a pretty steep accusation to make."

"All I know is what I hear," he said. "Certain noises. I'm sorry. She wasn't alone."

"How certain are you?"

"Dead certain," he said.

A few days later, reaching for our earplugs underneath the bed, I found a chain necklace instead: Johnny's chain necklace.

"So you've been sleeping with Johnny," I said to my wife.

When I confronted Johnny the next time he came round, I took him completely by surprise; "I thought you were looking for your *own* Amelia, not *my* Amelia!" I said to him; he cried like a wailing child, failing to catch his breath, his face overwhelmed by snot.

"Your punishment," I said, "is to tell me the whole story, point by point, detail by bloody detail."

12

I've complimented you on this face before. Many times. In the beginning you were surprised, as if you couldn't imagine yourself to be beautiful, or as if it was surprising to you that *I* might think it even though certainly many men had, but you were in love with me, so perhaps it was the mutual attraction that you found difficult to believe. Over time, I told you that you were beautiful but you had begun to question it—you thought that I was lying, saying so as a reflex, because I'd complimented you on your face before and as your husband was contractually obligated to. But I found you beautiful. I always have. And you believed me before.

I often remember a night at a pub in Richmond, during the first fortnight of our relationship, when someone, who'd just broken up with a guy, asked what the best reason for breaking up with someone was:

Infidelity, someone said.

How about: You don't *like* them? someone else said.

Amnesia, you offered. (I was so pleased you had involved yourself in the game.)

Halitosis.

Gonorrhoea.

That's curable now.

Ok, chlamydia.

Curable.

Herpes?

You fancy her sister, you said.

You fancy her mum.

You fancy her grandfather, I said.

Drug trafficking conviction.

To beat the other person to the punch.

I'm going to have to go with bad smells.

An *increased frequency* of bad smells, I added.

Infidelity with otters.

Canker sores.

That's oral herpes.

Hates animals. (You and I exchanged a brief glance.)

Hates children.

Hates people.

Likes children.

Likes people.

Terrible in bed.

Terrible in bed but thinks they're really good in bed, you contributed.

Really bad at English.

You mean, they're from some other place?

No, I mean, they're born in England but really bad at English.

Boring—they're a really boring person.

Tory.

Labour.

Australian.

American.

English.

Paedophile.

Yes, definitely if he was a paedophile, you said...

On the day that you left, I sat in this apartment we'd shared, rolling dough—I must have made twenty little mounds, all of which lay all over the place in tins or bowls, covered by towels, that later I'd freeze—tears in my eyes rolling down my cheeks, drying before they reached my chin, thinking that my reason for ending our marriage had been the very first on this list, that we'd ended because of a cliché, and that I was a hypocrite, because how many moments of infidelity had I already acted out in my head?

It's up to you, you said.

You said you were sorry, but that you also felt that marriage was imperfect. Not *us.* Marriage. I told you I understood, that I agreed. You told me not to blame Johnny. He'd honestly thought we were in an open relationship, you said (he'd assumed that we were in an open relationship the way we'd assumed that he, and his entire generation, were in them), but *you* knew what you were doing, and you'd even absolved him of responsibility by telling him it was okay.

I listened to what you had to say and left the apartment, wandered through Queens in the light of bodegas, in pain not because of the affair (so grandiose a word) or the cold, but because I felt so numb, so dulled, and I wished my reaction made sense. On repeat in my head were the words, *I've complimented you on this face before.* I didn't understand what they were doing there.

I understood your pain, how you did everything you could to help me forgive you—I forgave you immediately, I really did—but I saw the whole thing from a neutral, distant, almost narcotized position. What I couldn't understand was *myself*, why I was choosing distance, our mortal enemy, how had our connection snapped as a result of something so feeble (infidelity: a cliché…)?

I tried to make it work. I sat next to you in the morning in silence that became chatter, and boiled water that you would miraculously turn into tea. I told myself that it could have just as easily been me, but that you would have forgiven me. I sought to make you laugh, and we played records, and the soundtrack of the apartment remained as it always had.

But something unseen had been broken. What was it? I remember you saying that the present generation dared to do things horrendous and arbitrary because they believed that everything could be undone, that nothing could be erased and you could always go back a step by pressing the undo button. That's why, perhaps even more so now than ever, it always left an incredible sting when you realised something essential was dead, never to be retrieved again. Or is it simply that some things die without a cause, without explanation? That some endings come out of nowhere?

It saddens me to think that our life together ended so abruptly, so inexplicably. But now that I have the gift of time and perspective through which to see things, what you did—I didn't realise until much later—was liberate me. I could never cheat on you; it was against my design. *You* had to cheat on *me*. It was the only way out of this moral, the only loophole, the only way I could slip free into something else.

You see, we'd never transcended the beginning, the first year, of our relationship, which had been the best part. If you're honest with yourself, you'll agree with me—it would never be as good again as it was in the start…(And what a fantastic one, the stuff of life, of love…) The only way I could release myself from our marriage was for you to let go.

We could have spent the rest of our lives together, and we might have been happy. But, now that you'd opened the door, it was my turn to gamble on an even greater happiness. I didn't truly realise it until much later but, you see, I had been in love with someone else for some time. I didn't realise it was *love*—how could I have?—until much later.

I didn't realise it could be a love much greater than ours.

13

When I next saw Johnny Allan, eight or nine months had passed since Amelia had packed up her things and moved to New Orleans. He'd disappeared in a flash the day after I discovered their brief affair, finally taking in a single afternoon the long-overdue step of moving out of his father's house. He was late, and when he arrived I'd just come back from the bathroom, where there were intricate instructions describing how to wash one's hands (eight steps, with pictures), which I immediately shared with him (step one: "wet hands with running water…"), explaining that Amelia would have adored it.

"The temperature should be at least a hundred degrees, to kill off the bacteria," he said.

"That's right…" I said, remembering. "The dirty world…What's new with you?"

"I'm on a totally different toothpaste now," he said.

I laughed. I was impressed. It was the first time he'd ever answered any question I'd asked ironically. (Or was it the opposite: was this as literal an answer as you could get?)

"I'm sorry, man," he said, looking directly into my eyes.

"It's okay," I said. "Amelia told me you thought we were in an open relationship."

"It doesn't matter," he said. "I should have articulated it. I assumed so because it seems like all of y'all are in open relationships." He glanced over at the TV—"I don't know how anyone can stand these talking heads. I usually don't go to places where they have TVs turned on."

"Rachel isn't into open relationships either," I said. "You had that wrong, too. She was breaking up with you, but you didn't realise it."

"Really?" he said, looking off into the distance as if he were seeing that remote conversation.

"I was in love with her," I said, after a moment.

"I know, man," he said.

"No, I mean with Rachel."

"You were in love with *Rachel*?" he said, shocked.

"Well, at least I know that I was very, very attracted to her. I held back because I knew that I couldn't," I said. "That you're not supposed to cheat on your wife. As much as I would have liked to."

"I think you should call her," he said, after a moment's contemplation. "You'd be a much better fit for her than I was."

"Maybe," I said.

But I didn't. Another two or three months would pass before I'd see her by chance, walking down Hudson St. in the West Village.

"I was blown away when Amelia told me," she said, before I could say nearly anything else.

"It was just as surprising to me."

"And with Allan. I told you not to trust him."

"Did you say not to trust him?"

"If I didn't, I'm pretty certain it was implied."

"I saw him a few days ago," I said. "He quit his job at the pizzeria. Now he's working at a clothing store. He's still trying to save up money to get out of New York."

"Why would you see him?"

"I don't know," I said. "I guess I could never really blame him."

"Ignorance as a defence, it's rubbish," she said. "I would have beaten the shit out of him," she said. "Or fucked his girlfriend."

"Or even his ex-girlfriend," I said before I'd even understood what I was saying.

"Yeah," she said, and I looked her in the eyes to see if she'd understood, too.

"I've got to go meet a client right now. Give me a call," she said. "We'll meet for a drink, and then maybe I can help you out with that. Are you working today?"

"I quit my job," I said. "I rented some commercial space, remodelled it and opened up a pizzeria. It's called Gisela's, after my grandmother. She was a baker. You should come by," I said, handing her a flyer for the grand opening.

I'd let my facial hair grow and fashioned my moustache into a handlebar. From a clothing shop online, which sourced from restaurants and designers around the world, I bought a vintage white baker's outfit, shaped like a tunic (or a kurta), with white buttons that flanked the side, and a baker's hat that looked a bit like a newsboy cap, but was white.

The decision to leave behind the UN had come down to a few specific events. All the talk of Johnny's future and passion eventually led me to question whether I was passionate about my own choice of career. When I went to the conference in Germany, I found myself suddenly immersed in my parents' world, among intellectuals and academics, among those who were passionate about their work and those who were passionate about themselves, neither of which I wanted to be. I sat in a large auditorium listening to the discussions of work, the incestuous self-sustaining cross-referencing and politically-motivated annals of academia...Had my parents been in the room, the effect would have been different, and I wouldn't have noticed this. Their absence from the room effected in me an instant jolt of clarity: I wasn't living my own life. Sometimes you don't realise a song is playing over and again on repeat; you're distracted, your body is pulled in some direction, the song (and the force) is so faint as to be indistinguishable from the tug and pull of the earth.

I asked Aminata if she wanted to display some of her photos—she could sell them, I told her—and we went through some 20,000 of them to select those that captured best the mood of the place, of the neighbourhood, of this part of Queens, of faces recognizable to the customers that might as well be of them, of their relatives and family and friends and some of the characters of the street, the loitering recurrent faces that everyone knew. Online, we scoured the local global village for people advertising old frames, looking specifically for black ones (the future was black-rimmed and transparent…the clear glass was a lens through which one could, unabashed, stare back at the world). Using our Zombie devices, we mapped out a course that led us to an apartment building in Bellerose, a garage in Bushwick, and a co-op in the Upper East Side with an expensive view of Queens, but it wasn't until we were on the return trip, walking down Roosevelt Avenue that we came across a stoop sale and found exactly what we'd been looking for: several dozen metal frames, many of them broken or splintered, in black and bronze, rustic, weather-beaten and gorgeous.

One day I woke up and saw Aminata sleeping beside me. It was a Sunday in early autumn, when one peels off the sheets of his bed to feel a chilled breeze blowing through. Her trademark expression of scepticism and doubt lay on her face even in sleep, as if even her dreams were subject to the same scrutiny, and her lips were slightly parted, and thousands of small goosebumps lay across her bare bum like indentions made by porcupine quills. She shifted and turned into the heat of the blanket, her lips against my face.

She slept like no-one I've ever met, succeeding at both ends of the night, waking when well-rested, checking out when tired; awake, she was calm, nothing roused her to hysterics, and it impressed me how people made excellent subjects for her camera's lenses but not often for discussion afterward. Or: she never spoke generally about people but about specific persons; this was not her specific philosophy or something she even understood herself, and perhaps it is something one could only notice having been married to an Amelia. Aminata didn't spend much time paying attention to other people at all—or, again, her camera did, and this was enough—it's interesting how hypercriticality requires a certain distance, and thus alienation from life, thus even the hypercriticising of social distance requires itself a shade of distance.

I missed Amelia, too, at times, and I missed this hypercriticality, but Aminata's inner peace extended to me, calming the restlessness in my soul, and I realised soon enough that she didn't have any of the rough edges the constant *I-can't-believe-you're-stupid-enough-to-think-that* look on her face implied, which shielded her often from such stupidities and a number of situations other people got inadvertently tangled up in.

She taught me Fulani, which I seemed to hear everywhere once I'd begun learning it, and we visited Guinea eventually (and were stranded there for an extra week when typhoons called *doulourous* in Fulani turned Conakry and the outer prefectures into cities of dust), I ran the pizzeria, and in

February of '19 we were married at the downtown Manhattan city courthouse, the same year 1923 came roaring back.

14

"Can I take you into my confidence?" my future brother-in-law Denis said one day when we were sitting on the stoop, a few days after Johnny had left for Beijing.

"Of course," I said.

"I've had high cholesterol for years," he said.

"Oh," I said, after I'd understood what he was saying.

"As you can see," he went on, "*I* couldn't live with his mother. My good fortune was that she left me. I didn't want Allan to leave because I wasn't finished raising him yet. And I knew the effect of living with his mother. I couldn't put that on Allan. No-one should have to endure her sense of entitlement."

We wouldn't hear from Johnny for several months. He no longer had an email address, and he didn't like using the phone. The only way you could contact him was through expensive retro technologies like regular post, or by bike messenger or everything short a carrier pigeon. Perhaps remembering my wife's story about how she accepted my marriage proposal, he telegrammed when he arrived in Beijing.

When contact did come, it was in the form of several letters, addressed to each of us and arriving over the period of several days. This was mine:

Dear Alan,

I've spent the entire day rummaging through my thoughts. What is the next step? What will the next place I stay be like, the next woman I fall in love with, my next best friend or new companion (will he be a Chinese version of yourself?). Where will I find myself after the next book I read? Last week I was in Shijiazhuang, captivated by the mountains, exotic animals and the smells coming from a stove...

Outside I hear the city of Beijing, formerly Peking, Yanjing, Dadu, Beiping and Jingcheng...: hammering dough with long hammers, the televisions blasting in the adjacent building, some yelling, an orchestral sound coming from somewhere that I still don't know what it is, traffic (did you know they have traffic jams here that last nine days?). Yesterday, I left my room (tiny place with a bathroom in the hall shared with students and a few families) around six a.m. feeling guilty because the day before I stayed in the room the whole day. I took the train to Dazhongsi and walked through the streets to look at some graffiti I'd seen photos of, then I met some guys on bikes who spoke a few words of English, and I asked where I could buy a cheap one. They took me to this guy's house and sold me one for 150 yen, and then I just started riding around like a kid on a Huffy. I rode around until night, until I eventually saw water glistening in the distance, and was driven toward the suffusive flush of light reflected by the fading sun. I originally thought it was a fountain or something like that, but when I got closer I realized it was the Shichahai lake (you never think of lakes when you think of China), and I saw a girl, a beautiful girl, sitting on the side of the lake alone with the kind of smile on her face that would make you die to belong to her in some way.

The people in the apartment across from mine might tell you that I am an obsessive-compulsive, paranoid freak. I get up every minute, almost on the minute, to get some water, check a dictionary, wash my hands, go to the bathroom, pace dramatically…and so on. But to them it probably looks like something schizophrenic, like multiple personalities coming and going in seconds, fast.

Someone, this guy who turned out to be from Nanjing, saw me pulling out hand sanitizer for the 57th time in an hour and said there was some ancient Chinese remedy that could cure this. I asked around and found this guy, who had a kind of office in this place next to a gift shop, this place that sells all kinds of stuff including live turtles or fish on key rings. I told him my problem, and he waited for me to finish speaking, but he didn't say anything. I asked him if he understood what I was saying. He said, 'When does your problem start?" (Here no-one ever uses the past tense for anything.) I gave him my answer. He said, "I have a phone," and pulled it out of a drawer next to him. "That's great, man," I said. I left not long after that.

It got me to thinking. I have OCD, I'm one of those people you hear or read about. How the fuck had I missed that all of those years? If I hadn't broken my cell phone, I may never have noticed one of the most basic things about myself. And what else might I have missed? Now, I don't even remember what it was like: to have a cell phone, to hold it, to pull it out of your pocket, to check it, to type something out, to put it back, to pull it out again a few seconds later, or to never put it away, to have it in your hands always. What do I get in exchange for this loss of connection to the human race, for being a man outside of my generation? Time, Alan. I have nothing but time.

Or maybe my OCD is just a replacement tic. I used to get phantom vibrations in my leg. The phone rang even when it wasn't ringing. I'd check my pocket to see that nothing had come through. But there's still an echo of it in my body, an interruption. Then I realized: the obsessive need to wash my hands isn't my birthright—it's the leftover vibrations of addiction.

I think of you all the time. I think about your marriage and how I ruined it. I think about the time before that, before Jean-David, some of the happiest days of my life. I feel like here I'm starting over fresh, that maybe everything that's happened since meeting you and Amelia has been leading here, where my life can begin. And now it's time for me to start asking your question, What am I going to do?

I don't know.

Here I go again. It's all about me, isn't it? If selfishness is truly inseparable from our DNA or what it means to be human, why do I feel like I have so much of it and yet all the people I admire have so little?

Now is the time for less talking and more listening.

Abruptly I conclude this letter, with the promise of more.

"Johnny Allan"

P.S. If you want to write me back, make a photocopy of the address and just glue it on the envelope in the right place.

P.P.S. I always wanted to write a letter with a P.S.

I wrote him back, but received no reply, and several more months would pass before we heard from him again. This time he wrote to his father, telling him that he'd found work teaching English to children, four and five, in a rich family, that it paid the bills, he was learning Pekingese and he'd met a 19-year-old girl named Jia Li, a pedicurist who'd given him a pedicure (which he'd gone to get because of the dirt lodged inside his nails), and he was in love—with the money he was making, he'd bring her with him at Christmas; they were already looking into her VISA and the paperwork, and the bureaucracy involved would be a pain, but it would be worth it. This was the last we've heard from him, but that was only a few months ago.

And what of Amelia?

About a year after we split up, I downloaded some episodes of a talk radio programme onto my phone and was listening to one of them one day in the kitchen at Gisela's when I suddenly heard her voice saying, "Let's face it. Woody Allen shouldn't have a monopoly on *all* of 20s jazz, something that is *everyone's* inheritance. You don't know how many times I suggest a 20s song for the score of a film, and then someone vetoes it because they think it sounds too much like a Woody Allen film. And I *love* Woody Allen, don't get me wrong... I once fell in love with a guy named Alan and, seeing his name as an auspicious sign from the universe, married him." *Dear God!*

In the days leading up to 2019, she would become something of a celebrity—she'd gain quite a cult following among nostalgics and collectors and hipsters (and their French counterparts: the bourgeois bohème), talking on television chat shows and breakfast hours and inside magazines about this new rebirth, this renaissance that was, as she said, just around the corner. It seems people had been unhappy and had been waiting for something like this for some time—for 21 years, she specified, explaining how the release of all of this music into the public domain had been postponed in America in

1998 and quite luckily so—because, had the 20s returned then, during the last gasps of the golden age, they might have come and gone without anyone noticing. No, we needed saving *now*. Wherever you looked, you saw signs of it; the future was here and with it what was looking more and more like erosion and decay.

But oh how the organism resisted! You should have seen the way the people were dressed: wearing fedoras, cloches and top hats, flaunting their flapper dresses, carrying prohibition-era growlers, frequenting speakeasies. (I looked out one night to see *two* Ford Model Ts gliding nonchalantly down the avenue…) Could people foresee what was coming? (They were dressed for it.) Did they know what they were wearing? *Did it matter?* Here was its soundtrack, and with it, the promise of a new mould of human being, backlit by 20s jazz. (She'd said it herself—you lay a soundtrack over the image and turn it into something else.)

But we were due a great era, weren't we, after all the nonsense of the past several decades that made everything seem so grotesque, like a nightmare slept through, like the promise of youth that had never arrived, of a Time and a Generation Lost; *here* it was, and she would be the one to deliver it—it seemed both greatness and the future belonged outright to her—this syncher of sounds, unlocking the time capsule to a spreadsheet of great, hibernating tunes and carols and the pleas and poetry of the past (of dreams, *visionary gleams*, deferred).

Here it was and would be, a new era, one that would rekindle the past, the future that would belong to the likes of Johnny Allan (and to Algernon and to Samuel, and to me…), synched to his story as it unfolded, that would be here now any moment, on a flight in from Beijing (dressed how? with what amount of greatness clinging to his breast?)

Here it was once again: an encore performance this very evening, of something that we all thought had disappeared and expired or been lost; here *finally*—in a stranger's hat, dancing upon the fire escape, in the rising heat of the New Year, a *vision*, a scene of incomparable beauty and self-love, a film version of reality composed of the best fragments of the past and, in the background, under the noise of the times but beginning now to rise from the ashes and the dust and slumber: its tune, its timeshattering score!

A SAMPLING OF MUSIC TO BE RELEASED INTO THE PUBLIC DOMAIN ON JANUARY 1, 2019

"The Charleston"—Arthur Gibbs and His Gang

"Dizzy Fingers"—Zez Confrey

"High Society Rag"—King Oliver's Creole Jazz Band"

"Down-Hearted Blues"—Bessie Smith

"Dippermouth Blues"—King Oliver's Creole Jazz Band (with Louis Armstrong)

"Wolverine Blues"—New Orleans Rhythm Kings

"Milenberg Joys"—New Orleans Rhythm Kings

"Tain't Nobody Business If I Do"— Bessie Smith

"Marchéta"— McNalpak's Dance Orchestra

"Dreamy Melody"—Art Landry

"Tin Roof Blues"—The Original Memphis Five

"I've Got The Yes! We Have No Bananas Blues"—Eddie Cantor

"Yes We Have No Bananas"—Ben Selvin Orchestra, featuring Irving Kaufman, vocalist

"Come On, Spark Plug"—Arthur Lange And His Orchestra

"Love Sends a Little Gift of Roses"—Carl Fenton

"I'm Sitting Pretty In A Pretty Little City"—Lou Davis, Henry Santly & Abel Baer

"Bambalina"—Paul Whiteman and His Orchestra

"Só Teu Amor"—Orquestra de Eduardo Souto

NOTES

I wrote this book over the course of a month in August and September '13. Or it was mostly written then, but a few pages, ten or so, were there already from a few months before. The point being, this book was breathed into being in a very short period of time, and thus aims to capture a small sip of life that for me represents the mood of those days, and the mood of the times I so hoped it might corporealize.

This book is dedicated to Jonathan Duran, Peter Rae and Sara Verhagen, a trio of artists whose work and thoughts and friendship have influenced me in unquantifiable ways, aside from being ideal companions along that long, tumultuous road that is an artist's life, a life that, despite the occasional and essential creative solitude, is one meant to share. Jonathan lends his image to the cover, and so to the book; while early readers and mutual friends say they can easily picture him in the role of Johnny, well, that was my intention: that he one day *play* Johnny in the film version. But the character of Johnny Allan is, as perhaps only fellow artists will believe, a fiction: a symbol, as characters in stories are, of real-life figures known and unknown, shadows of people passing through this incipient century as it seeks a ledge on which to perch before it, too, flies away!

Aissatou Diallo and Fatoumata Diallo—I appreciate your help scrutinizing my references to Guinea (any errors that persist I claim entirely for myself), entertaining me with songs like Halima Bah's "Forsa Djomba," and teaching me—over the past year—words such as "jarama" and "owo." *Owo, bimbi*, my dear Diallos!

The few words in Fulani here are transliterated, and I've made decisions, occasionally, to write such things as, for example, what is sometimes rendered "djarama," "jarama." Without a standardized Latin spelling, one gets to choose.

November '18

about the author

John M. Keller is the author of four other books of fiction, and multiple screenplays. Visit his website, knowyourbaker.com, for additional information.

ALSO AVAILABLE FROM DR. CICERO BOOKS

THE SECRET NAME OF NOW BY ROBERT KELLY

A poet of the greatest powers with a devotion to our art and to the shared life from which it springs second to none in my memory.—Jerome Rothenburg

FORGETTING BY FIRAS SULAIMAN

In Syrian poetry, Firas Sulaiman stands alone.—Khaled Khalifa
One of the most significant Syrian poets in the world today.
—James Byrne

ASMITA BY SENEKA ABERYRATNE

Abeyratne's command of prose is technically brilliant. *Asmita* is a timely criticism of a cross-section of Sri Lankan society.
—*Sri Lanka Daily News*

CHEROKEE ROAD KILL BY CELIA BLAND

Cherokee Road Kill is an important book written by a poet in total command of her craft.
—Jonathan Blunk, *The Georgia Review*

HOW TO PUSH THROUGH BY CAREY HARRISON

As thorough an examination of postwar European consciousness as Thomas Mann's *The Magic Mountain* was of its era.—*American Library Journal*

TIGER BY ASHLEY MAYNE

Mayne's prose is ferocious and lovely. This is a haunting story that confronts the spaces in which violence and beauty meet.
—*Foreword Reviews*

THE LOST TRAVELLER BY STEVE WILSON

There's a writer here, beneath the blood-boltered leather.
—Martin Amis

Thoughtful, funny, savage and sexy. —*Time Out*

OTHER BOOKS BY JOHN M. KELLER

A BALD MAN WITH NO HAIR

Mesmerizing short stories that take the reader from Mexico to Russia, to Chile, to the Far East, and back.

KNOW YOUR BAKER

A world-famous painter from El Paso is dead. Or has disappeared. He's left behind a final piece of artwork that doubles as a suicide note—and may contain clues.

THE BOX AND THE BRIEFCASE...

Brazil's film industry is shaken to the core when its most famous citizen flees and is killed; her niece, poised to become its next great star, seeks to explain her mysterious death.

ABRACADABRANTESQUE

Americans abroad, snug in Montevideo, Uruguay, until their investigative reporter pal Felip, in trouble in North Africa, needs their help.

For more poetry and fiction titles, visit us at www.drcicerobooks.com.

To the memory of my beloved mentor, the distinguished Brazilian educator, Dr. Emanuel Cicero, born in 1907 in Ubatuba, São Paulo. Rector of the College of Rio Grande do Sul from 1943 to 1978, he died in 1988 in Lisbon.

–Maximiliano Reyes, publisher

-FIM-

Made in the USA
San Bernardino, CA
09 January 2019